"You encouraged Daniel to fall for you as part of your job, Ms. Dorsett. You can guess what we call that kind of woman in Glory."

Lori faced Ann. "That wasn't my intention."

Ann kept talking. "You know what really bothers me, Ms. Dorsett—you've hurt a lovely man, a wonderful pastor."

How could she explain to Ann what had actually happened? How could she try to justify her job?

She jogged down the hallway, eager to get out of the church. Once again, doing her job had caused someone pain.

It comes with the territory. People don't like you to discover their dirty little secrets. Except, this time is different.

This time, the bad guys were mostly good guys. And this time, Daniel Hartman was at the center of the situation.

This time, the ░░░░░░░░░░░░░ *asy to soothe.*

Books by Ron and Janet Benrey

Love Inspired Suspense

Glory Be! #55
Gone to Glory #67

RON AND JANET BENREY

began writing romantic cozy mysteries together more than ten years ago—chiefly because they both loved to read them. Their successful collaboration surprised them both, because they have remarkably different backgrounds.

Ron holds degrees in engineering, management and law. He built a successful career as a nonfiction writer specializing in speechwriting and other aspects of business writing. Janet was an entrepreneur before she earned a degree in communications, working in such fields as professional photography, executive recruiting and sporting-goods marketing.

How do they write together and still stay married? That's the question that readers ask most. The answer is that they've developed a process for writing novels that makes optimal use of their individual talents. Perhaps even more important, their love for cozy mysteries transcends the inevitable squabbles when they write.

RON & JANET BENREY

GONE TO GLORY

Steeple
Hill®

Published by Steeple Hill Books™

STEEPLE HILL BOOKS

Steeple
Hill®

ISBN-13: 978-0-373-44257-7
ISBN-10:   0-373-44257-2

GONE TO GLORY

Copyright © 2007 by Ron and Janet Benrey

www.SteepleHill.com

Printed In U.S.A.

My conscience is clear, but that does not make me innocent. It is the Lord who judges me.
—*1 Corinthians* 4:4

For our brothers and sisters in the "Souper" Life Group at New Spirit Community Church.

ONE

Lori Dorsett let her rented sedan coast to a stop close to the curb on the eastbound side of Oliver Street. Without looking left or right—or at the map of Glory, North Carolina, on her lap—she knew that she'd parked opposite Founders Park and up the street from Snacks of Glory, "the home of the Glorious SOGgy Burger." Another fifty feet or so and she'd be able to see the garish red-and-yellow neon hamburger glowing in the restaurant's window.

"You do good work," she murmured happily, confident that she'd learned the lay of the land. She'd memorized the locations of the small town's landmark buildings: the town hall, the police headquarters, the fire department and the Glory National Bank.

And of course, Glory Community Church.

Immediately after breakfast, Lori had driven every one of Glory's fifteen major streets at least three times—and many five or six—but in a random pattern to relieve suspicion should anyone be watching.

Like the lady cop on Main Street who decided that I was casing the bank.

Lori chuckled. It was too bad that she didn't have her camera with her at the time. Lori would have loved to

capture the look of disappointment on the cop's face
when she realized that Lori was a tourist in Glory and a
guest at The Scottish Captain.

Later in the morning Lori had driven through Glory
again, visiting the town's best-known historic sites and
buildings to take pictures, actually going to the trouble
of unfolding her portable tripod and snapping shots from
various angles.

Photography was the heart of Lori's cover. She'd supposedly just finished a year-long certificate program in travel
photography at the Chicago Institute of Graphic Arts. Her
camera—a professional-quality Nikon digital single-lens
reflex—was larger and more expensive than most tourists
would carry. And she had a complete assortment of lenses
and filters and memory cards—exactly the sort of extrava-
gant camera system that would be owned by a well-heeled
recent divorcée striving to transform a hobby into a new
career.

Founders Park would be Lori's last "photo shoot" of
the day.

She climbed out of the car, crossed Oliver Street and
set up her camera in front of the statue of Moira
McGregor. The visitors' guidebook that Lori had nearly
memorized explained that Moira had been married to
Duncan McGregor, the leader of the group of Scottish
émigrés who had settled Glory in the spring of 1733.

"I'll be with you in a flash, Moira. Hold that silly grin
while I make a phone call."

Lori surreptitiously scanned her surroundings. There
were no trees in her immediate vicinity and the buildings
on the south side of Oliver Street were fairly low, yielding
a clear view of the sky.

She switched on her satellite telephone and dialed Kevin Pomeroy's direct line in Chicago.

"A happy Tuesday morning to you, Mizz Dorsett," a cheerful male voice boomed. "How's life in the Southland?"

"Quiet. It's the middle of a workday here and there are maybe a half dozen cars on the street."

"What were you expecting? I warned you that Glory is a clone of Mayberry."

"You were right, Kevin. I keep waiting for Andy Griffith to walk around the corner. I've seen ten different women who look like Aunt Bea."

"Where are you staying?"

"Where we want me to be—The Scottish Captain."

"Ha! I told you we didn't need to risk making a reservation."

"You were right again. The place has six bedrooms. They won't fill up until the summer."

"Watch out for bedbugs."

"To the contrary. The Captain is a grand old house— lovely inside. The sort of place you should take Francine for a romantic weekend." She laughed. "The town has a definite charm about it, too. There are several excellent restaurants, I've been told."

"Uh-huh. I'm sure that the art museum is inspirational, and I'll bet the local galleria has an impressive collection of Fifth Avenue boutiques."

"Well, cultural opportunities are somewhat limited, but I have passed a few interesting specialty shops."

"Right! And there's always the big box stores on the outskirts of town." He moaned. "I almost feel guilty sending you to a hick town—until I remember that your last assignment was two months in San Francisco." He added. "Do you have any sense of how long you'll have to sojourn in beautiful downtown Glory?"

"Three weeks, maybe four. To be on the safe side, I told the owner of the B and B that I planned a month of picture taking in the region."

"How's the weather?"

"The month of May in this corner of North Carolina is *glorious*. No pun intended."

"What's that supposed to mean?"

"Half the businesses in town have names that start with Glorious or Glory. To give you an idea, there's the Glorious Burger, the Glorious Table, the Glorious Dry Cleaner, the Glory Girls Shop…and my favorite—Snacks of Glory."

"Speaking of business…have you run into the lawyer yet?"

"Yep. She helped me carry my bags up to my room. I recognized her immediately—she looks exactly like her photograph. Plump. Blond. Early sixties. Attractive."

"This is *too* easy." He chuckled. "You're not going to tell me she's in the bedroom next door, are you?"

"Nope. Apparently there's a good-size apartment on the third floor of The Scottish Captain—she lives up there."

"Good. Stay out of her way—she's a sharp cookie."

"So am I."

Lori listened for his reply. When none came after about ten seconds, she asked, "What's wrong?"

"I'm worried about you. I hope you're taking proper security precautions."

"Of course I am. For starters, I'm calling you on a satellite phone. No one in Glory can eavesdrop on the signal." She readjusted the chunky device against her ear. It was a size larger than many of the latest cell phones;

anyone watching would assume she still owned an old cell phone from the late '90s.

"I wish you had a gun," Kevin said. All the usual humor had left his voice

"I don't need one." She added, "These are church people—a bit crooked perhaps, but not organized criminals."

"Yeah, but I still wish you had a weapon. There's already been one murder related to the case."

"On that happy note, I'll say goodbye."

"Watch your back, Lori."

"I always do."

She turned off the sat phone and thought about Glory Community Church—the epicenter of everything that had recently happened in Glory. She peered up at Moira McGregor's smiling face. "First I'll take your picture," Lori said, "then I'll drop by the church to see whom I can meet."

Pastoral care was not among Reverend Daniel Hartman's chief spiritual gifts. He knew that he could preach and teach with gusto, but neither expertise was especially useful when a longtime member of Glory Community Church wanted his hand held, his back patted and his anguish comforted.

When in doubt, let them talk it out.

"You we're saying that you feel guilty…" Daniel prompted the man seated at the other side of the round table in his office.

"*Worse* than guilty." George Ingles shook his head slowly. "I feel incredibly stupid. I can't begin to understand how I let this mess happen. I've failed everyone in the church."

Daniel managed to quell his urge to nod in agreement. He concurred with George's harsh self-assessment. The man had been a world-class pinhead; he'd let the whole congregation down. And now the church was in dire straits because of the poor decision he had made.

"I'm sure," Daniel said, "everyone at Glory Community has forgiven your…ah…misplaced confidence. You put your faith in a man who didn't deserve your trust. Anyone might have made the same mistake."

George stared at the floor. "I'm not *anyone*. I've had enough experience to know better. I should've spotted the warning signs."

Daniel grunted noncommittally. George went on. "The fact is I don't think anyone at church has forgiven me. Forgiveness is tough—especially when you have to forgive someone who lost close to a million dollars of your money."

Daniel merely nodded. What could he say? George was right. In his role as Glory Community's financial secretary, it had been his responsibility to invest the church's nest egg wisely. The year before, John Caruthers, a member of the choir, had left the church a six-hundred-thousand-dollar cash bequest and ten rare books that the church had sold for more than $350,000. In keeping with John Caruthers's wishes, the gift would be used to support the music ministries at Glory Community and other less affluent churches.

But now the money was gone. George had been conned by a man named Quentin Fisher, a supposedly Christian financial adviser of impeccable reputation. Quentin had worked at McKinley Investments Ltd., a stock brokerage of equally sterling repute. Quentin had talked George into making a series of risky investments that promised to double the church's money in a few months. Four months later the church's investment account had been wiped out—and Quentin was dead.

"And our plans and dreams for the wonderful music ministry are gone," Daniel muttered to himself.

He glanced at George. Perhaps he should tell him the truth—that George knew less about finance than he thought he did. True, he had an M.B.A. and had been a vice president in a large corporation. The more important fact was that George had worked most of his career in human resources and had hardly any day-to-day experience managing large sums of money.

Daniel couldn't bring himself to do it. "With God's help, everything will be set right," he said. "We have a good chance of winning our lawsuit against McKinley Investments. I have high hopes that we'll get our money back."

"Me, too. But who knows how long that will take? What do we do until then?" He rolled his eyes. "We made commitments to assist three poor churches. They are relying on us to help them, but now we don't have the money to make good on our pledges. What are we going to do about that? I don't have the heart to tell their pastors that we're broke."

"We must lean on God and muddle through the best we can."

"I suppose so—even though I hate to think of myself as a muddler."

Daniel looked up in response to a gentle tapping on his open office door. The church's administrative secretary, Ann Trask, strode into the room, a determined expression on her young face. Daniel stifled a smile. Ann often seemed twenty-four going on forty, a petite blue-eyed blonde who would have made a great drill sergeant. In fact, Ann oversaw the daily business of Glory Community Church with startling efficiency. Daniel had come to rely on her intelligence and discernment.

"Yes, Ann," he said.

"There's a woman here—a visitor to Glory—who wants to photograph our stained-glass windows from the inside of the church…" She seemed to end her sentence in midthought.

"And?"

"I was going to say okay, but—" she sighed "—with everything that's happened recently, I decided to make sure that you don't mind."

Before Daniel could respond, another person appeared in the doorway. "Perhaps I had better explain why I'm here, Reverend Hartman."

Daniel looked past Ann in surprise. His unforeseen visitor struck him as extraordinarily pretty—a woman worth staring at. Her brown eyes seemed bigger than most, her mouth fuller and her nose better proportioned. She had brunette hair cut fairly short and a dark complexion. The woman stepped around Ann and into his office.

Out of the corner of his eye Daniel saw George Ingles leap to his feet. Daniel stood, too.

The woman walked toward them, her right hand extended. "My name is Lori Dorsett," she said. "I'm from Chicago—I'll be visiting Glory for the next month or so." Daniel noted that she moved gracefully, but with the kind of powerful grace achieved by an athlete rather than a ballet dancer. "I'm staying at The Scottish Captain."

He felt a twinge of annoyance when George—on the

side of the table nearest to Lori—moved next to her more quickly than he could and lunged at her hand. "I'm George Ingles," he said, voice oozing, "an elder of the church and our financial secretary. Let me welcome you to Glory. We like to think of ourselves as the friendliest small town in North Carolina."

Daniel tried to take charge. "Friendly indeed, Miss Dorsett, welcome to Glory," he said enthusiastically. "The Captain is one of our nicest bed-and-breakfasts." But his words had no effect. George Ingles maintained his grip on Lori's right hand and she seemed content to keep smiling at him.

Why would she feel that way? Daniel wondered. George was your run-of-the-mill, sixty-year-old retired businessman, slightly overweight, mostly bald and totally married. There were hundreds more like him living in Glory. Lori, by contrast, was a rarity in town—a stunning woman in her late thirties with a splendid figure and a bare ring finger.

Daniel tried again. "I take it that you want to photograph inside our sanctuary, Miss Dorsett?" he said, significantly louder this time.

Her smile faded as she turned toward him. "I'd hoped to begin with some outside photos," she said, "and then, with your permission, to move inside the building." She made a vague gesture in the direction of the sanctuary. "Your stained-glass windows are really quite lovely."

"You have a good eye. Our five windows were imported from Scotland in 1858. They were designed by Daniel Cottier, the famous Scottish stained-glass artist, and crafted in the equally famous glass studios of James Ballantine, of Edinburgh. Each window illustrates one of Jesus' parables."

He let himself grin. "See if you can deduce which parables when you photograph the windows."

"I'm afraid I haven't opened a Bible in more than twenty years. I'm not sure if I even remember where to find the parables of Jesus."

"Then you don't belong to a church back in Chicago?"

She shook her head. "Sorry—I haven't thought of myself as a Christian since I was fourteen years old." She added, "I hope that won't disqualify me from taking pictures inside your church?"

"Not at all. Our sanctuary windows have been one of Glory's attractions for more than a century and a half. We're delighted that visitors want to take pictures— regardless of their beliefs."

"Thank you," she said. "I appreciate your understanding."

George Ingles jumped back into the conversation. "You might feel differently about your Christianity if you attended one of our Sunday worship services." He beamed at her. "Our choir and our praise band are first-rate—the finest in Glory. And Daniel, here, delivers a pretty good sermon."

"I have to admit that I'm tempted…" she said. "I promise that I'll think about it."

George patted Lori's shoulder. "We can't ask more than that, now, can we?"

"It was lovely meeting you," Lori said to George, and then to Daniel, "Thank you, once again, Reverend Hartman. I promise that I won't be a nuisance."

Daniel returned a halfhearted wave to Lori as she left, then glanced at George, who was clearly waiting for Lori to be out of earshot before he said anything else. A moment later the church's heavy front door swung shut.

"It's the story of my life," George said with a mock display of anguish. "The ladies love me, even though I never disguise the fact that I'm married. I tell you, Daniel, it's a curse."

Daniel knew that his friend was joking, but he still felt another round of annoyance at George's delight. Why did Lori act the way she did? What did George have that he didn't?

Enough! Stop thinking like a jerk.

Daniel took a deep breath and wondered why he felt the way he did.

TWO

Emma Neilson glanced at the clock above The Scottish Captain's aging stove and felt a flutter of excitement cut through her rotten mood. Noon! In less than ten minutes she would look out the kitchen window and see Rafe—her husband of scarcely two months—marching along the flagstone path behind the Captain.

Rafe, I need a hug. Badly.

Rafe's job as Glory's deputy police chief required that he work long days, often stretching into evenings. Her job as owner and proprietor of The Scottish Captain put her on duty at about six every morning. Their daily lunches together were an oasis of calm during the middle of their twelve-hour workdays that they both could enjoy.

Emma banged a stoneware plate on the small table in the kitchen, fully aware that she was taking her annoyance out on the crockery. Most lunches she could talk about pleasant things with Rafe—but not today. Her morning of shopping in Glory had been decidedly disagreeable. She'd been glared at by three different people—two of whom she didn't even know.

Ill will toward her seemed to be growing worse with each passing day. It had started a week earlier when Rafe had arrested Tony Taylor for the murder of Quentin Fisher. Many of Glory's upstanding citizens thought that killing Fisher, a big-city stranger, was a fabulous idea, a fate he richly deserved for defrauding Glory Community Church and trying to con Tony Taylor. They resented Rafe, and Emma, for doing his duty.

Emma glanced at the cover of her latest marketing brochure, fresh from the printer. Her marketing communications firm had sent over the first dozen copies. The photo on the cover, one of her favorites, captured the Captain on a crisp fall day when the trees had reached the peak of color. White letters above the photo proclaimed, "The Scottish Captain: A Charming B and B in North Carolina's Friendliest Town."

Friendliest town, my foot.

The clock inched closer to twelve-ten. Emma checked on Calvin Constable's latest culinary experiments, which had begun to bubble nicely in the microwave. Calvin, her breakfast chef, was an inveterate innovator, whose latest project was to develop a series of hot entrées that combined North Carolina cuisine with international dishes. The dish in the microwave was Southern Fried Thai Chicken. Well, how bad could it be?

Emma turned the brochure over. The back cover illustration was a stylized map of Perquimans County that made the town of Glory seem larger and more important then Hertford, the county seat.

The kitchen door flew open and Rafe entered, his cheeks rosy from a fast walk from police headquarters. Her heart sang to see him looking so happy. She hurried over to hug him and be hugged. After a long welcome-home kiss, Rafe sniffed the air. "Chicken?"

"Mostly," Emma replied. "It's covered with peanut sauce that's flavored with a mix of Thai and Southern spices."

His face registered mild surprise. "Calvin strikes again."

"I made us sweet tea to go with it," she said. "With a touch of cardamom to echo the Thai theme."

Rafe poured himself a glass of tea. "Mmm. Delicious." He added after another swallow, "How's your day going so far, my love?"

She sighed softly then said, "You'll probably wish you hadn't asked, but I've had better mornings. The Send-Rafe-Neilson-a-Nastygram team was hard at work on the streets of Glory."

"Sorry about that." He shook his head. "What can I say, except that's what small towns are like?"

"The scary thing is that two people I don't know joined in the fun. They must have recognized me from the picture of us that ran in the *Glory Gazette*."

"Have I told you how beautiful you look in that photograph?"

"Don't change the subject. Jacqueline Naismith—a member of our choir—buttonholed me on Main Street and gave me a ten-minute overview on what she thought about you arresting Tony."

"I suppose it's natural that folks in town are mad at me."

"Actually, they're mad at *us*. By some weird logic, I became responsible for the actions of the police department when I married you."

"I'm sure people will soon calm down."

"I'll bet they don't, Rafe. It will be months before Tony goes to trial. We'll be castigated until all the facts come out." She shook her head. "'Thou shalt not kill'—

except when someone cheats your church out of a small fortune, then it's 'be my guest.'"

Rafe took her hand. "That's not what's going on. Really! Most people are angry that Tony was denied bail and is stuck in jail. They blame the police, although we didn't have anything to do with the judge refusing bail. That's almost inevitable with a charge of first-degree murder."

Emma felt herself shiver. "I cringe every time you say 'first-degree murder.' I find it hard to believe that Tony Taylor murdered anyone, a belief I apparently share with most of Glory's upstanding citizens."

"There's a mountain of evidence that says he killed Quentin Fisher. I had to arrest him."

"I'm sure you're right…" Emma hesitated. What more was there to say?

Rafe took another sip from his glass. "I really like what you've done with the tea. I expect the Captain's guests will, also. Will you offer it to them?"

She shrugged. "Bed-and-breakfast guests prefer coffee and hot tea to start the day. Iced tea is a drink best suited for the afternoon."

"How many guests do we have this week?"

Emma bit back a smile. She hoped that Rafe would grow to love The Scottish Captain as much as she did. Every "we" he spoke encouraged her. "A total of five," she said. "A couple from Virginia Beach, a couple from Washington, D.C., and a woman from Chicago who's practicing to be a travel photographer."

Rafe picked up one of the marketing brochures that Emma had left on the table. "Now here's a fine example of excellent travel photography—I like this picture of the Captain."

Emma nodded. "Me, too. The old building never looked better."

The photo had been taken nine months earlier, a few days after the three-story wooden structure with its large windows, deep porch and wide front steps had been newly painted. Emma had chosen the color scheme carefully: cream for the clapboards and cornflower-blue for the wooden shutters and trim work. The eye-catching double oaken front doors, both freshly varnished, provided a lovely accent. The dressed-up inn looked solid and imposing, just the sort of house a Scottish captain might commission for himself in 1895—assuming he wanted to build an elegant residence for rich single women. That was the building's original purpose.

"However…" Rafe tapped the back of the brochure. "You forgot to change your last name to Neilson. This says, 'Emma McCall, Proprietor.'"

Emma grabbed a brochure, horrified. Her new brochure would have to be reprinted. She shuddered at the thought of what it would cost. "Nice catch," she managed to say. "I should have let you be one of my proofreaders."

Emma felt a surge of relief when the microwave dinged. Serving lunch would take her mind off the defective brochure. She took the lid off the casserole. "This smells good," she said, serving up spoonfuls of chicken. "It looks peanuttier than I expected."

"I like peanuts." Rafe held out his hand, Emma took it. "Lord, thank You for the food and for all Your bounty," he said. "And thank You for Calvin, who never ceases to amaze us. Amen."

Emma tasted a forkful of the new dish. "Hmm. I'm not

sure I can eat this. It tastes…*odd*. Perhaps Calvin used too much lemongrass."

Rafe took a bite and promptly made a face. "By any chance do you have the makings of a grilled-cheese sandwich?"

"A wonderful idea." Emma leaped from her chair. "Two grilled-cheese sandwiches coming up."

She found a package of sliced Swiss cheese and soon had two sandwiches grilling in a heavy cast-iron skillet. "This won't take long."

The inside kitchen door opened without warning and Christine Stanton's head appeared. "Something smells delicious," she said.

"True." Emma gestured toward the casserole full of Southern Fried Thai Chicken. "But Calvin's latest experiment tastes like an explosion in a spice shop. We're going to have grilled-cheese-and-tomato sandwiches instead." She smiled. "Want to join us for lunch, Christine?"

"Thanks, but I have a lunch date with Daniel Hartman and George Ingles at Glory Community Church." She beamed at Emma. "This is first time since I retired that I get a chance to offer legal advice. I'm looking forward to being a real lawyer again."

"Ah. The lawsuit against McKinley Investments."

"My one and only case," she said.

Rafe shifted his chair so that he could see Christine without straining his neck. "How goes the battle?"

"It goes slowly," Christine replied. "My big problem is the alleged murder of Quentin Fisher. Because of that, McKinley Investments is taking their own sweet time responding to our letters of complaint. I presume that their lawyer is telling the firm to wait until all the facts come out at Tony Taylor's murder trial." She looked up happily. "I think we can speed things along by encouraging the McKinley firm to settle."

"Are you sure you can't have a sandwich with us?" Emma said.

"Nope. I heard voices in the kitchen and dropped in to say hello—but they expect me up at the church, because I'm bringing lunch." She punctuated her words with a salute-like wave. "Gotta go."

Emma waved back. "See you later." She kept waving as Christine let the kitchen door close behind her.

"That woman is a gift from God," Rafe said.

"Both for the church and me," Emma said.

Emma had married Rafe knowing they faced a difficult problem. When she moved to his charming house with its fantastic view of Albemarle Sound, there would be no one on duty at night at The Scottish Captain. No one to admit late arrivals or guests who'd lost their keys. No one to call in case of an emergency. No one to provide an extra blanket or pillow or towel to a guest who needed one.

And Emma had no choice but to move: the Captain's third-floor owner's apartment was simply too small to accommodate three people—especially when one of them was a lively teenager. Kate, Rafe's fifteen-year-old daughter had her own bedroom—and her own bathroom—in the charming blue-clapboard Victorian bungalow on Front Street that Rafe owned.

Christine had checked into the Captain a month before the wedding, told Emma she was in the process of moving to Glory, and asked where she might find an apartment in town. Emma quickly offered her the Captain's owners' apartment at a remarkably low rent—

with one stipulation. "You'll be the Captain's night manager," she'd explained. "Your duties will be simple. Help the guests when I'm not here."

Christine agreed immediately—and had proven to be ideal for the job.

Emma lifted the cooked sandwiches from the skillet and joined Rafe at the table. "Do we need to say thanks again?" she asked.

Rafe began with a big smile. "Thank You, God, for grilled-cheese-and-tomato sandwiches, and for not requiring that we eat Southern Fried Thai Chicken. Amen."

Rafe took a bite of his sandwich. "Perfection!"

"I agree. We should frame these sandwiches rather than eat them."

"Speaking of frames…" Rafe said. "Tell me about the fifth guest—the gal from Chicago who's driving a blue rental. The one who wants to be a travel photographer. Is that why she spent the morning driving around Glory?"

Emma nodded. "She's assembling a portfolio of photos of the Albemarle region."

"I'll tell Angie Ringgold that she's not a master criminal. Angie was on patrol this morning. She saw the rental car looping back and forth through Glory. She said that she followed the car down Main Street at least five times. Angie really got suspicious when she saw it slow down in front of the bank."

"Did she intercept the driver?"

"Angie was about to stop her car, but then it surprised her and drove to the Captain. The driver went inside and came out carrying a bunch of camera gear. Angie last saw her taking a picture of Moira McGregor in Founders Park."

"Poor Angie." Emma laughed. "For your information,

the lady's name is Lori Dorsett. She's from Chicago. I don't know much about her, except that she was divorced last year and is trying to launch a new career as a travel photographer. She plans to stay in Glory for a month or so and take a lot of pictures."

Rafe took another bite of his sandwich and washed it down with a gulp of spiced iced tea. "Angie told me that the gal is a real looker—is that true?"

"I wouldn't know," Emma said airily.

"Wow! She must be gorgeous."

Emma balled up her napkin and threw it at Rafe's head.

It had been a snap decision—but an inspired one, Lori thought—to tell Reverend Hartman that she wanted to take pictures of the stained-glass windows from outside the church. Now she was perfectly positioned on the church's lawn, adjacent to King Street, to listen in on the meeting in the pastor's office.

Lori reached deep into her oversize black-leather camera case, into a small compartment near the bottom. The gadget she found resembled a plastic candy bar but was the single most expensive item in the bag. It was a bugging device—a remote sound monitor—that could surveil a room a hundred yards away. She began to mount the innocuous-looking gadget on the top of her tripod.

Her hand slipped. She caught the remote sound monitor before it hit the ground.

Easy girl. You're still shaking.

Lori inhaled slowly, counted to five and then exhaled. She'd almost lost her composure when, without any warning, she was introduced to George Ingles in the reverend's office. She hadn't expected to run into the one person in Glory she absolutely, positively had to meet. And amazingly he had turned out to be a flirtatious jerk.

Perhaps that will come in handy someday?

Two more gifts of fabulous luck. In fact, things were going almost *too* well. When would the good fortune run out?

Lori drove the unpleasant thought out of her head and asked herself a more productive question: what were George and the pastor meeting about?

She immediately offered herself an answer: the church's finances. What else would Daniel Hartman have to talk about with George Ingles?

"You'll know for sure in about thirty seconds," she murmured, "if you can get this silly gadget working."

Lori tried again to attach the tripod's screw to the bottom of the remote monitor. This time the threads engaged; she tightened the screw gently and made sure that the working side of the device was pointed toward Reverend Hartman's window. She knew that there were two nearly invisible lens openings on the front edge. One lens had an infrared laser behind it, the other a sensitive optical detector.

The device was really quite simple in principle: it directed an invisible beam of infrared light at the pastor's office window and picked up some of the light reflected off the glass. The cleverness of the device lay in its ability to detect tiny vibrations of the window glass caused by the sound waves generated by people talking inside the room.

She placed a small earpiece in her left ear—the same kind of wireless earphone that many cell phone users wear—and activated a small switch on the bottom of the sound monitor. Now came the tricky part: she would have to aim the laser beam at the pastor's window while non-chalantly appearing to do something else.

She picked up her camera and stared at its controls while she slowly moved the tripod's pan and tilt head.

Lori's earpiece came to life. "...she'll be here with lunch soon, George. She's bringing sandwiches from Snacks of Glory. I like them even better than their burgers."

A burger would taste terrific about now.

Lori abruptly felt hungry. She wished that she had bought a Glorious SOGgy Burger when she had the chance. All she had with her now was a half-eaten granola bar and a small bottle of water. They would have to do until the meeting was over. The conversation going on in the pastor's office was far more important than her hunger.

"Then maybe we should talk about a special steward-ship campaign before she arrives." Lori immediately identified the speaker as George Ingles. It was easy to tell him and the pastor apart because Reverend Hartman's voice dripped with authority. What else would you expect from a man who had been a U.S. Army chaplain for more than twenty years and had risen to the rank of full colonel?

She recalled the brief encounter in his office. Daniel Hartman also moved with authority, and he was better-looking than any clergyman she could remember—not that she had dealt with all that many men of the cloth. She had his photograph—a large color shot of him in his full dress Army uniform—safely stored in her laptop computer, along with the rest of the dossier that Kevin Pomeroy had provided. Hartman was forty-eight, but looked much younger. He was over six feet tall, fair-complected, with lively hazel eyes and a full head of reddish-brown hair. He had grown up in Nashua, New

Hampshire, earned a bachelor's degree in philosophy from Dartmouth, a master's in theology from Gordon-Conwell and, more recently, a doctor of ministry degree from Erskine Seminary. He had also earned two Purple Hearts, one in Panama, the other in Iraq, where he'd been wounded during the first Gulf War. Lori recalled the details from the dossier Kevin had provided and chuckled to herself. She probably knew more about the good Reverend Hartman than most of the members of his congregation.

His powerful voice filled Lori's ear again. "Well, you're our financial guru, George. The church's Elder Board will agree to do what you recommend. Do you really think we need a special campaign?"

"Yeah, unfortunately we do. Hopefully, a special fund-raiser will replenish enough money to let us pay the bills and honor the pledges we made those poor churches." He added, "I foresee only one hitch. Our members might hold back their giving if they haven't forgiven my mistakes."

Lori snorted. Forgive George Ingles? *I would have booted him out of the church building.* He'd made some truly stupid fast-buck investments for the church, but it was hard to determine whether he should have known better.

Lori flinched as a voice behind her said, "Hi, Lori. How goes the picture-taking?"

Lori felt her surveillance training kick in. She willed herself to turn around slowly, seemingly without concern or surprise. She simultaneously took a step away from the tripod. A moment later she was gazing at Christine Stanton's smiling face.

"It's too soon to tell, Christine. I'm trying to figure out which lens and filter combination I need to photograph the stained-glass windows. After I take the outside shots, I'm going to shoot them from the inside."

"Well, have fun."

"I always do." Lori noticed that Christine was carrying a shopping bag labeled Snacks of Glory.

Christine Stanton was the "she" bringing the food to the meeting.

Lori watched Christine walk toward the church and forced herself not to look at the remote sound monitor on the tripod. Instead she made a show of rummaging in her camera case among her various lenses and filters. She could hear walking and shuffling sounds in her earpiece, but no voices. What were Daniel and George doing? she wondered.

"Hey! What are you guys doing next to the window?" Christine's voice boomed through the earpiece. "Don't tell me! You're watching our pretty new visitor take pictures. Since when did you two become dirty old men?" She began to laugh.

"She's certainly worth looking at," George said.

"Uh-huh," Christine said. "I promise that I won't tell Margo what you said or recount the excitement in your voice when you said it."

"Ah…she told us that she's from Chicago and staying at the Captain," Daniel said. "Do you know anything else…uh, interesting about her?"

"Wow, padre! She got to you, too."

Lori resisted a powerful urge to look at Daniel Hartman's window. Was he still staring at her?

Christine kept talking. "Well, I know that Lori Dorsett was recently divorced and that she probably took a bundle of money from her ex, because she has enough fancy photographic equipment to open a shop. She claims that she wants to be a travel photographer. I've no idea why she started with Glory as a subject, but she's been taking pictures all over town. I haven't seen any, so I don't know if she's any good. Maybe I'll have an opportunity to see her work later."

"Not a chance!" Lori muttered. She had a story ready to respond to any requests to look at her photos. *Sorry, but I never let anyone see my raw digital photographs. I'll be delighted to show you the final results after I've had a chance to edit and crop them.*

"Your instincts are good," Daniel said. "What do you think about her?"

"I think she's a trophy wife who's coming out of a bad marriage and is trying her best to start fresh. She's a little ditzy, but that's not her fault."

Lori ignored a sudden pang of unease. She never felt comfortable when people bought her lies "hook, line and sinker," like Kevin—a committed fisherman—loved to say. It seemed too easy to lie to good people—they trusted you, assumed you were telling the truth.

Well, Lori Dorsett was one of the "good guys," too. Her investigation would ensure that justice was done in the upcoming lawsuit. All eyes were focused on McKinley Investments—but no one thought about the insurance company that stood behind the firm. If McKinley Investments were forced to pay damages to Glory Community Church, the money would come from the Chicago Financial Insurance Company. As one of three investigators in the Loss Control Office, Lori had the job of making sure that the claims were legitimate.

Why are ordinary folks so willing to cheat insurance companies?

It was a question that Lori had often asked herself during her three years on the job. In assignment after assignment, she'd seen "honest people" file false claims. Every new investigation made her more skeptical, more willing to be suspicious of everyone involved in the case.

Mistrust is an occupational hazard for someone with your abilities.

Lori took pride in her surveillance and investigatory skills. She had acquired them during a twelve-year stint as a special agent in the U.S. Army's Criminal Investigation Division. The formal photograph of her in a dress-blue warrant officer's uniform looked just as soldierly as the picture of Colonel Daniel Hartman that currently resided in her computer.

Too bad he'll never get to see the photos side by side.

Lori's earpiece blared once more. "Who ordered the egg salad on rye?" Christine asked.

"That would be me," George said.

"Then you must be the pork barbecue on a roll, with all the trimmings."

"Guilty as charged, Counselor," Daniel said.

Lori heard a stream of crumpled-paper sounds—followed by a series of chomping noises—that made her feel hungry once again.

"We might as well get started," Daniel said. "Does anyone have anything new to report?"

"Well…" Christine replied. "First, I can report that I'm making good progress learning about securities law. I'm researching as fast as I can—this isn't the kind of law I've practiced before."

Lori sniggered. "That's nice to know."

Christine went on. "Second, I've verified that Quentin

Fisher had a great reputation. I haven't found a hint of other deceptive business practices anywhere in his long career. There are no other complaints against him. I wonder why he chose the church to begin his crooked practices?"

Lori murmured, "Now, that's an excellent question."

"I assume we'll learn why as our lawsuit progresses," Daniel said, "which brings us to the main item on our agenda—the lawsuit itself."

"Quentin Fisher," Christine said, "had a duty under the law to recommend *suitable* investments to the church. He breached that responsibility when he sold us excessively risky corporate bonds. We planned to spend the money within a year or so—we needed good, safe, short-term investments."

Lori retrieved a tablet computer from her camera case and began to jot down notes about what Christine said should some of it be useful later.

Christine continued. "The church signed a brokerage agreement with McKinley Investments that says all disputes between the parties will be settled through binding arbitration by a panel of arbitrators rather than a courtroom trial. The upside of arbitration is that it takes months instead of years. The downside is that we can't appeal a decision that goes against us. However, the great majority of advisor lawsuits are settled before arbitration begins. That's our goal."

"And ours, too, honey," Lori muttered. She adjusted her earpiece, which had slipped out of the center of her ear.

THREE

Daniel Hartman hated prisons. During his years as an Army chaplain, he had visited prisoners in dozens of Army stockades. His trip to see Tony Taylor in the Albemarle District Jail, in Elizabeth City, took him to his first civilian lockup, but he knew exactly what to expect: the clank of steel doors, the embarrassment he felt as he passed through the metal detectors, the harsh lighting in the green-painted meeting room that would give him a headache, the smell of sweat that seemed to permeate the air, the hint of disinfectant and the oppressive atmosphere that he knew would stay with him long after his return to Glory.

Daniel put up with it all because Tony had changed his mind and requested his visit. At first, Tony had wanted no one but his lawyer to "see him caged up," as he put it. But yesterday, surprisingly, he had sent a message via his lawyer: "Please visit ASAP. I need your help."

Daniel had mentally prepared himself by praying for thirty minutes in his office and again during the drive along State Route 34A. But he was still surprised by Tony's appearance. Daniel felt a wrench of anguish to see Tony, who usually wore fancy vests and cashmere sweaters, dressed in a prison jumpsuit. The big man, a retired naval officer, seemed to have diminished in size. Worst of all, his expression seemed beaten down and more than a bit hopeless.

"Hello, Tony," Daniel said. They were required to sit on opposite sides of a small metal table. "No hand-shakes," the correction officer had said. "No contact." The officer had left them alone, but he was watching through a glass panel in the door.

"Thanks for coming," Tony said. "You don't have to sugarcoat your words—I know I look like an abandoned shipwreck."

Daniel decided to go along with Tony's wishes. "I'd ask how you're doing, but your appearance speaks volumes. You look like you aren't sleeping well."

Tony's shoulders sagged. "I mostly lie awake at night thinking about the Glory at Sea Marina. The work's got to be piling up. I can't expect my wife to do it for me. Rebecca puts in backbreaking hours at the hospital." He shook his head. "If I don't get out of here soon, I'll lose my business."

Tony slapped his palm against the tabletop. The noise reverberated through the small room. "I shouldn't be here. I didn't kill Quentin Fisher. I had nothing to do with the accident at the marina."

Daniel nodded, not sure what to say.

"Ask yourself this, Reverend. Why would I want to kill Fisher? He hadn't succeeded in cheating me. All I cared about was getting the church's money back. For that, I needed him alive, not dead." He held up a finger. "But…if I had wanted to kill the skunk, why would I choose a method that put my whole marina at risk? The explosion could have easily started a fire that engulfed all of the

docks." He held up a second finger. "And another thing—
I'm not stupid. Why kill Fisher in a way that calls attention to me?"

Daniel nodded again. Everyone in Glory had theories
about the "accident," as Tony called it. The facts, such as
they were, had been widely reported in the *Glory Gazette*
and on local TV stations.

Three weeks earlier, Tony's personal boat—an elegant
23-foot-long classic wooden runabout named *Marzipan*—had exploded at Tony's marina. There wasn't any
uncertainty about the explosion itself. Gasoline vapors
had collected in the bilges and inside the boat because of
a leaking fuel line. A random spark had ignited the vapors
and triggered the explosion. The real mystery, however,
centered on why Quentin Fisher had been sitting in
Marzipan's cockpit when the small boat was consumed
by a fireball that shot more than fifty feet into the air.

Quentin Fisher had become Tony's financial adviser a
few weeks prior. All their dealings had been over the telephone or in the conference room in the McKinley Investments office in Greenville.

Quentin had no reason of his own to travel to the Glory
at Sea Marina on the day of the explosion. He was there
because Tony had sent him an e-mail inviting him to the
marina. The police had subpoenaed Tony's Internet
records and had found a copy of the e-mail in the "Sent
Messages" directory on Tony's computer.

Tony interrupted Daniel's musing. "I can see the
wheels in your head turning, but none of the so-called
evidence that I killed Fisher is right. I didn't send him that
e-mail. It was sent on the Thursday afternoon before the
accident—but that's when I was out in Albemarle Sound

testing the rebuilt engine in a big motor cruiser." Tony added, "And I certainly didn't send him a faxed map of the marina."

Daniel didn't see the point of arguing with Tony, but what could explain away the evidence that the police had? The marina's telephone records showed that—also on the previous Thursday afternoon—a one-page fax had been sent from Tony's fax machine to Quentin's fax machine. Moreover, an employee at the boatyard saw Quentin Fisher walking on the docks a few minutes before the explosion. Quentin approached him and asked for help finding a boat named *Marzipan*. The employee noted that Fisher'd had in his possession a faxed diagram of the marina's docks.

Tony rested both hands flat on the tabletop. "And let me tell you the most relevant fact of all. *Marzipan* was worth a fortune. She was my pride and joy: I'd rebuilt her personally. Who in his right mind would destroy a genuine antique to kill a slime ball like Quentin Fisher?"

Daniel nodded once more. Everything Tony said made sense, but then, each of the prisoners he'd visited over the years could spout a dozen good reasons that proved his innocence. Most of them would conveniently ignore an especially strong fact or two. Tony hadn't mentioned the garage-door transmitter.

When arson investigators from the Glory fire department—supplemented by two evidence technicians from the North Carolina State Bureau of Investigation—sifted through the debris, they found a radio-controlled detonator in the remains of *Marzipan*'s bilge. The detonator had been built using a garage door remote-control system. The police, acting under a search warrant, rummaged through Tony's office at the marina. They found a matching garage-door transmitter tucked behind a row of books on his bookshelf.

Daniel found it difficult to look Tony squarely in the eye. He didn't want to believe that his friend was guilty of murder, but the evidence seemed...well, "overwhelming" was the word that Rafe Neilson had used. Daniel had had a heart-to-heart talk with Rafe, who had been remarkably forthcoming.

"I wish it wasn't so," Rafe had said, "but all the evidence points to a simple fact. Tony Taylor turned *Marzipan* into a bomb that killed Quentin Fisher."

Daniel had countered, "For what purpose? What was Tony's motive for killing Quentin?"

Rafe had thrown both hands up. "The obvious one, of course. Tony figured out that Quentin Fisher was cheating the church. We found a letter to Fisher outlining his alleged fraud in Tony's computer. The letter demanded that McKinley Investments return the church's money."

Daniel had pressed. "Okay, but why kill him?"

"Because Fisher refused to return the money," Rafe had said. "We figure that Tony decided to kill Fisher in the hope that his 'accidental death' would clear the way for McKinley Investments to take a fresh look at the church's failed investment."

Daniel had chosen not to argue with Rafe. After all, what could he offer as an alternative theory? But Rafe's reasoning as to Tony's motive seemed awfully weak. Would he really kill Quentin Fisher as part of a revenge-driven scheme to get the church's money back? That didn't seem anything like the Tony Taylor he knew.

Now, as Daniel observed Tony's distress in jail, he

wished he had at least challenged some of Rafe's assumptions. He should have pressed Rafe, made him explain more.

"I'm curious…" Daniel said. "What led you to Quentin Fisher in the first place?"

Tony shrugged leisurely. "I guess I foolishly assumed that George Ingles knew what he was doing." He let his head roll backward, then forward. "Look, Rebecca's uncle died six months ago and she received a cash bequest of about a hundred and fifty thousand dollars. We were looking for an aggressive investment—something a bit riskier than usual that would have high returns. I asked George for his advice. He referred me to Quentin Fisher. I admit I was very impressed that he worked for McKinley Investments."

"And he asked you to send him a check?"

"Not quite. At first he didn't want to talk to me. He said that he handled major accounts and he offered to turn me over to one of the more junior investment advisers."

"And?"

"I said fine. A few days later Fisher called me back and said that he'd be happy to take on my account." Tony gave a mirthless laugh. "*That's* when he asked me to send him a check."

"And did you?"

"No. I dragged my feet. I wanted to see what kind of investment he would suggest before I made a commitment." He grimaced. "I was astounded by what he came up with. Como Creative Media is a real dog. He tried to convince me that their corporate bonds would go up—I knew better."

"But George Ingles didn't?"

"I guess not."

Daniel wanted to dig deeper, but decided not to. Any more questions about George would verge on gossip. Instead he asked, "So you never actually invested with Fisher?"

"Nope." He paused. "When I realized that Quentin Fisher was a hack, I took a close look at the bonds that Fisher had sold the church and I confronted him about them."

"Why didn't you tell anyone else at the church what you were doing?"

"Two reasons. I didn't want to embarrass George, and I didn't want to cause a panic among the congregation. I thought I'd be able to get the money back without making a big fuss." He added, with a smile, "Feel free to use my story if you ever need a good example of foolish pride."

Daniel returned the smile. When he was sure that Tony had nothing more to say, he asked, "How can I help you today, Tony? Besides praying for you, of course."

"I need someone in my corner. Someone who cares enough to find out what really happened that day. The cops think I killed Quentin Fisher, so they've stopped investigating. I need someone who still has an open mind. I need *you*, Daniel."

"Me?"

"My defense attorney recommended that I hire a private investigator, but it would take a month to bring him up to speed and a year to get folks in Glory to cooperate with him. Even then, he wouldn't really care about me. I need you."

Daniel thought about arguing with Tony—until he saw the determination in the man's eyes. Tony would not take no for an answer.

"You've given me quite a challenge," Daniel said. "Of course I'll help in every way I can—including praying for you."

Tony's expression darkened for a moment but then he said, "You do that, Reverend. And while you're praying, imagine what's going to happen to me if you can't help me prove my innocence. I'll spend the rest of my life in a prison far grimmer than the Albemarle District Jail."

Daniel shivered at the notion. There was indisputable fear behind Tony's plea for help. And cold logic in his description of what could happen to him. For the first time in decades, Daniel began to wonder if prayer was enough.

Okay, Mizz Dorsett. It's time to begin your scheming.

Lori slipped her camera case under her bed and retrieved her laptop computer, the smallest and thinnest portable available. She switched it on and opened a password-protected file that contained comprehensive dossiers of George Ingles, Christine Stanton and Daniel Hartman.

"A big hello to the Big Three," she said. "Eeny, meeny, miney, mo. Which of you is best to know?"

Lori scrolled to the bottom of the document, then back to the top, stopping awhile to look at a large photograph of each "candidate." One ofthem would soon be her weak link at Glory Community Church—the person who would, with gentle prodding, be encouraged to share information about the ongoing lawsuit.

She moved the cursor next to the photo of George Ingles and let herself smile. Her easiest target might well be flirty George, the fellow who started it all by making foolish investments. She'd probably learn a lot of delicious details from George—but would it be possible to befriend him?

The information that Kevin had gathered about Ingles was inconclusive. He held a bachelor's degree in elementary education and a master's of business administration. He had taken a job in what used to be called the personnel department at a small software company and eventually became vice president of Human Resources for a high-tech conglomerate.

Despite his blustery self-confidence, George might well turn out to be an all-talk-no-action type of man, the sort who panics if his flirting actually works.

Lori tapped the Page Down key, to a small photograph of a pinch-faced woman in her late fifties. To make matters worse, George was married. Margo Ingles had been his secretary for many years before they married, so she'd be achingly familiar with his coy antics. She probably kept George on a short leash and would work hard to terminate an unexpected relationship with a newly arrived woman more than twenty years younger than her husband.

Lori ran her finger along the computer's touch pad and placed a red highlight atop George Ingles's name. "Sorry, George," she said. "We'll never know how great our relationship might have been."

Lori scrolled down the page to Christine Stanton's photo and felt her smile fade into a frown. It would be hard work to sidle up to Christine. She was one of those women who wanted to believe the new divorcée in town was a pretty but brainless ditz. Lori remembered the puzzled look she'd received from Christine outside the church. It had spoken volumes.

"She was amused to see me taking pictures with a complex camera," Lori murmured. "She undoubtedly assumed that I'd have endless problems figuring out how to work the dials and controls."

On the other hand, maybe you're being too hasty.

Lori brought the cursor atop the photo so that the "+" rested on Christine's nose. Given the right circumstances, Christine might spill all of the beans to a "dumb but nice" friend. And as the church's legal advocate, she would know everything worth knowing about Glory Community's case…

No. She's much too bright.

That was the chief downside of getting close to Christine. The dossier explained that Christine Eloise Stanton held a magna cum laude degree in political science from Smith College and had graduated with honors from University of Virginia Law School. These days, she might be toting guests' luggage into the Scottish Captain, but that didn't take away her savvy or her smarts. If anyone could figure out why Lori had come to Glory, it would be her. The risk of making friends with her was too high.

Lori turned Christine's name red then touched Page Down to reach the one remaining candidate: Reverend Doctor Daniel Hartman, minister of word and sacrament, the pastor who had to deal with a nearly impossible mess. Daniel sat at the hub of Glory Community Church. He knew everyone involved with church finances and attended every meeting. He'd be more fun to be around than George and more forthcoming than Christine.

And the winner is, Daniel Hartman.

Lori studied his picture. Kevin had managed to find a lovely photograph of the pastor, although he really was so much better-looking in the flesh…

Knock it off, lady, you're on duty.

Lori chuckled. There was certainly a lot to like about Daniel Hartman. Besides being unusually handsome, his various degrees from Dartmouth College, Gordon-Conwell Theological Seminary and Erskine Seminary proved his intelligence. Equally important, he was charmingly polite and had an authentic knack for making people feel comfortable. Daniel had taken her put-down of Christianity in stride and seemed genuinely embarrassed by George Ingles's clumsy come-on. It was a shame that she'd decided not to acknowledge his annoyance back then. Keeping George happy had been more important to her than impressing the pastor.

Lori centered Daniel's picture on the screen. His eyes seemed filled with determination. She'd have to work extra hard to persuade him to share the information he had. Pastors tend to be close-mouthed, used to keeping secrets. Daniel looked even more resolute.

Lori wondered if she could also consider Emma Neilson—a B and B owner, recently married to the town's deputy police chief, and Christine Stanton's new boss. Lori quickly decided that she'd have to work too hard to become Emma's fast friend. *And once I did, she wouldn't have much information about the case.* Emma sang in the church choir, but that wouldn't automatically give her access to what Chicago Financial Insurance needed to know.

"Nope. My best candidate is Daniel Hartman," she murmured. "I can bypass some of his resolve with electronic surveillance gear."

Lori felt herself smile at the thought. She would supplement her one-on-one contacts with Daniel by installing a bug at the church. A combination of investigatory techniques would make sure she got everything she needed. *Better safe than sorry.*

Her satellite phone began to ring. She retrieved it from her handbag and moved close to the window to give the antenna a better view of the sky.

"How we doing this afternoon, Mizz Dorsett," Kevin asked, without any preamble.

"We're doing peachy-keen. Why do you ask?"

"This is usually the time in every undercover assignment when you have a mild attack of scruples. I thought I'd nip it in the bud."

"Yeah, well, I'm not having any second thoughts today. In fact, I'm making good process. I've just selected my Trojan Horse."

"Let me guess—George Ingles."

"Nope. Daniel Hartman, even though he's not a sure thing."

Kevin whistled softly. "The pastor! I'm impressed. And I'm also surprised. Isn't hoodwinking a pastor considered a heavy-duty sin?"

"Very funny."

"Okay. I'll get serious. You tend to get close to the people you investigate. That's what makes you a true undercover artist. But you also tend to take the sides of people you get to know. And that's when you can become a pain to manage."

Kevin's voice became softer. "You like the town of Glory. You respect the people you've met. I could hear it in your voice earlier." He seemed to hesitate. "You okay with all of this?"

"All of *what?*"

"If your investigation succeeds, the church won't get its money back."

"If I succeed, as you put it, it will mean that I've uncovered evidence that George Ingles made a rotten investment with his eyes wide open. That would mean that the church doesn't deserve to get its money back." She added. "And you're right—I do respect the people I've met. They're cheerful, direct and *nice*. I haven't met any phonies yet." Lori recalled George's sleazy sweet talk. "Well, maybe I did meet one phony." She added, "Anyway, I never take anyone's side."

Kevin snorted. "Speaking of rotten investments…we received another package of relevant documents from McKinley Investments. This stack of goodies includes the last monthly brokerage report that Quentin Fisher filed before he was killed. He claims that he urged the church not to buy junk bonds, but that the church's financial secretary wanted to maximize return and was willing to accept a higher risk."

"When did Fisher submit his last report?"

"The middle of April."

"That seems rather late in the day. The church invested the money in February. Quentin Fisher counseled George Ingles in January."

"I suppose he was finishing up his required paperwork—you know, dotting his i's and crossing his t's."

"More likely, Quentin Fisher was covering his tail. He wanted to document that he lived up to his responsibility to give the church sound financial advice—even though he probably didn't."

"Hmm. Didn't someone just tell me that Lori Dorsett never takes sides."

"I don't and I haven't," Lori said. "One needn't play favorites to recognize that something's wrong with Quentin Fisher's story. It doesn't ring true. We don't have all the facts on him. We don't know everything he did."

"Maybe so, but Quentin Fisher's not our problem. Our primary target is George Ingles." Kevin grunted, a signal that the debate was over. "To change the subject, I hope you're eating well. I'm concerned for two reasons. I need you to stay healthy and don't want you to return to Chicago with a craving for chitlins and cornpone."

"I'm eating very well, thank you. Since Chicago Financial Insurance is paying my expenses I intend to sample all of the best restaurants in Glory—the kind that have lobster and filet on the menu. In fact, it's approaching my usual dinnertime and I'm feeling a bit hungry."

"Bon appetit!" Kevin said with a laugh. "Let's talk again tomorrow."

"Whatever!" She pressed the disconnect button.

Lori turned off her computer and grabbed a lightweight jacket. Spring evenings could be cool in Glory. She ignored the stab of concern she felt as she left her room. There was a simple spring lock on her door, but every container in her room was unlocked: her suitcase, her camera case, her attaché case that held her computer and a folder full of travel brochures. This seeming indifference was in keeping with the laid-back persona she'd chosen. Christine Stanton would expect a "ditz" to behave that way. Better to risk a theft than raise unnecessary suspicions about herself. And besides, the odds of her room being burgled in a town like Glory were small.

As Lori walked toward the front door, she saw Christine sitting in the parlor, reading what looked like a thick law book.

"That's definitely heavy reading," Lori said.

Christine raised her eyes. "Out to take more pictures?"

Lori stepped into the parlor. "No. I'm in the mood for a short walk then a good meal."

"Well, you can't do much better than a stroll along the Glory Strand, down by the waterside. Turn left when you leave the Captain and take another left on Dock Street. Keep walking, you'll end up at the start of the Strand."

"Left, left and walk. Got it."

"When you get to the end of Dock Street, look to your right and you'll see the Glory at Sea Marina. There are a couple of fine seafood restaurants nearby. The Glorious Catch is big and fancy. The Fisherman's Inn is small and cozy."

"The Fisherman's Inn sounds perfect. I'm kinda gloried-out."

"Good choice. The Tuesday night special is usually homemade Maryland-style crab cakes."

"Yum!"

Lori had taken several small steps into the parlor during the brief conversation, bringing her close enough to Christine to read the spine of book she held: *Litigating Financial Fraud*.

Lori nodded at Christine and backed out of the room. She would have to track down the book on the Internet and find out if it was a text for beginners or experts. That would be a useful bit of information to know. But it certainly could wait until after she ate her fill of crab cakes.

FOUR

A soft thud against the outside of his closed office door made Daniel look up from the church budget spreadsheet he'd been studying. He'd been expecting Ann Trask to join him, but she *never* knocked before entering his office, which meant that he would have to deal with someone else before he and Ann could get down to productive work.

"Come in," he said, trying to keep the annoyance he felt out of his voice. More than a week ago he'd set aside the first two hours of this Wednesday morning so that he and Ann could quietly review the church budget and revise the figures downward.

The only answer was another thud.

"Come in," he said, more loudly than before. His prayer on waking at sunrise had been for discernment—but it took a clear, untroubled mind to be discerning. He felt on the verge of being angry.

A third thud sent him bounding from his chair, furious. He hurried to the door and flung it open. There stood Ann, holding a large tray that held a plate of homemade sticky buns, another plate of cookies, two mugs, a steaming carafe and all the usual coffee fixings. Her blue eyes twinkled. "Goodness, what took you so long to come to the door?" She pushed past him. "You'd better take this tray—it's getting heavier by the second."

Daniel took the heavily laden tray and realized that for the zillionth time in his life he had mistakenly over-reacted. It was his most vexing character flaw, the one he had to apologize for most often.

"I'm sorry, I wasn't expecting…"

"Of course not. I should have warned you, but I figured you could use a treat to help you deal with the budget. I know that you hate financial numbers." She smiled. "You told me that the first day I came to work."

"Ann, you're a gem."

"Keep that in mind. My annual evaluation comes up next month."

She pulled a visitor's chair close to the side of Daniel's desk. When he sat in his swivel chair, she dropped onto hers.

"I didn't tell you the whole truth just now," she said. "I woke up early and baked sticky buns mostly because I couldn't sleep. The idea of cutting our budget has me so depressed that I start crying whenever I think about it."

Daniel patted Ann's hand. "Whenever I feel that way—and I often do—I say, 'The Lord giveth, and the Lord taketh away. Even as it hath pleased the Lord, so cometh things to pass: blessed be the name of the Lord.'"

She frowned. "I know I've heard that before, but I can't think where it comes from?

"The Anglican Book of Common Prayer. The English have buried people with that phrase for many hundreds of years." He took her hand. "It's a simple reminder that everything we have is from God."

She returned a weak smile. "I do wish God would've let

us hold on to what He gave us a little bit longer. Having the money then not having the money makes my head spin."

"Mine, too. Well, let's pray before we go to work."

He watched Ann bow her head and then closed his own eyes. "Lord, we ask You to bless our efforts this morning. We have difficult choices to make and we know that we won't do a good job on our own. We ask You to give us discernment. Be with us to provide the help and counsel we need. We pray these things in Jesus' name. Amen."

He blinked his eyes open when he heard her speak a quiet, "Amen."

"At the risk of offending you some more, Ann, I think it's best that we both agree not to discuss our decisions with anyone else."

Ann began to pour coffee into a mug. "I agree. Budget cuts will be tough to swallow. People are going to get mighty stirred up when they learn their ministries aren't being funded."

"Fortunately, the final decision will be made by our able Board of Elders."

"Reverend, the Elders asked you to make suggestions so that they can agree with everything you suggest. When it comes to reducing spending, the ball is in your court." She added a spoonful of sugar to her coffee. "Anyway, most of the Elders assume that we're going to get our money back."

"I certainly hope we do."

"Hope? I thought it was a sure thing."

He shrugged. "Christine and George are confident, but there are no guarantees when you go to arbitration. McKinley Investments isn't a stupid company. They obviously think they can win."

Ann peered at him over the top of her mug. "Whew! The only reason the members haven't tarred and feathered George Ingles is that they expect us to recover what we've lost."

Daniel filled his own mug. Ann was exaggerating about the congregation's feelings toward George, but she had the Elders pegged right. Ultimately the board wanted him to craft a new budget. The Elders were smart enough to anticipate the "elbowing" that would happen if each of them fought to protect his own pet project. Better to let the pastor propose controversial financial solutions.

"Let's begin with our pledges," Daniel said. "If I recall, pledging is down from last year."

"About ten percent, Reverend. But I think that's to be expected, don't you?"

Daniel nodded. "Absolutely! Lots of our members have sent their tithes to organizations in greater need. After all, we were rolling in cash when our stewardship campaign began."

Ann's face brightened. "Maybe we could hold a 'second mile campaign' during the summer? We can give it a snazzy name, something like 'Step up Again.' Or…" Her shoulders sagged. "I don't know. Maybe I'm being impractical. I know that I'll have a hard time coming up with more money this year." She lifted her hands in a gesture that signaled the inescapability of her situation. "My old clunker of a car is on its last legs. I was even thinking of asking the church for more hours. I guess that's out of the question for a while."

"It looks that way," Daniel said. Eleven months earlier, Ann had agreed to work a twenty-five-hour week at Glory Community. Back then, everyone had expected her job to grow into a full-time position. Ann had returned to Glory to live with her ailing mother after earning a Bachelor's degree in business administration from East Carolina University. Her zeal and efficiency made the church run more efficiently than it ever had before. Daniel especially appreciated her no-nonsense attitude. He knew that every task she began would be done right. She'd amply proved her worth and deserved to become a full-time employee.

Ann is another casualty of George Ingles's foolish investing.

"Okay," he said, "gift-giving is down. Let's go through the budget line-by-line to see if we can find any obvious fat. We'll start with our planned spending for the church building."

Ann made a face. "There goes the new carpeting in our fellowship hall. I was looking forward to a nicer floor, but the old carpeting is still serviceable—even though it's tired-looking. The kids who play on the floor won't mind if we delay for another year.

"Agreed."

"We were also going to repaint the hall."

"Paint is relatively cheap, we'll leave it in the budget. After all, all the labor to do the painting will be provided by volunteers."

She grinned at him. "But now they will have to work extra hard to keep paint off the old carpet."

He returned her grin. He hoped they could maintain their good mood as they sliced and diced the rest of the budget.

Daniel lost track of time and was pleased to discover that they'd finished the budget review in less than ninety minutes.

"Okay," Ann said as they reached the budget's final

line item, "we've managed to trim eighteen percent out of this year's planned spending. I only see two really painful cuts."

"Where are they?"

She tapped the spreadsheet with her pencil. "We cut the funding for Vacation Bible School and our Christmas pageant by fifty percent. VBS can charge a small fee to make up the shortfall, but I vote that we restore the original budget for the pageant."

"I'm not sure I understand why pageant needs so much money this year?"

"They need to buy new wings for the angels. Half of our old wings molted on stage last December. Don't you remember?"

Daniel felt himself smile. He did remember. The congregation had laughed again and again as feathers fell every time an angel moved.

"Let's go for new wings," he said as he leaned back in his chair. Ann made a final note on her spreadsheet. She stood and began to gather the various plates and mugs on her tray. She abruptly said, "Reverend, there's another budget line item that could pop up later this year."

"What did we leave out?"

"Well…several members, me included, want the church to help Tony Taylor. We're worried that Tony and Rebecca will have to dip into their retirement accounts to pay for his legal expenses."

Daniel grunted in lieu of an answer. He knew that the Taylors could afford the significant cost of a skilled defense attorney and had hired a well-regarded law firm in Charlotte, but he wasn't at liberty to tell Ann about the recent bequest from Rebecca's uncle.

"Yes, indeed." Daniel tried to sound noncommittal. "I like the idea, but our decision can wait until we know more about Tony's circumstances."

She seemed satisfied by his proposed compromise. "Have you seen Tony lately?"

Daniel nodded. "As a matter of fact, I visited him yesterday." He didn't elaborate. Tony hadn't sworn him to secrecy, but why spread the word that he'd been asked to help prove Tony's innocence?

Ann frowned. "It must be awful being stuck in prison."

Daniel shuddered as he recalled Tony's gaunt face, hollow eyes and pleading expression. "Awful is the right word," he said. "We have to keep Tony in our prayers."

And I have to figure out how to keep the promise I made to him.

"What would a real detective do first?" he muttered.

Ann turned in the doorway. "Pardon me?"

He smiled at her. "Pay no attention—I'm blithering."

Daniel watched Ann leave his office and shut his door. *A real detective would probably find out the latest about the case.* Daniel reached for his telephone, dialed the business number for the Glory Police Department and asked for Rafe Neilson.

Daniel rolled his swivel chair closer to the open window at the side of his desk. The sky was clear and the temperature had climbed to the low eighties. A gentle easterly breeze blowing in from the Albemarle Sound carried a hint of the marshes close to shore. All in all, a perfect day to go fishing.

"Hello, Padre," Rafe said cheerfully. "What can I do for you?" He seemed, Daniel thought, in a good mood.

"I'd like to chat about Tony Taylor."

Rafe's tone changed abruptly. "I feared Tony might be the topic. I heard that you spoke with him yesterday in jail."

Daniel felt a jolt of surprise, but then realized how Rafe had learned about his visit.

"Ah. The jail keeps track of Tony's visitors."

"And they tell us." He hesitated. "Although we don't know what you talked about."

"I'll be happy to relieve your curiosity, Rafe. Tony asked me to help him prove his innocence."

Another hesitation. "How do you intend to do that?"

"I really don't know—yet. But it seems to me that the first step is to fully understand the case against Tony. I'd appreciate anything you can tell me without violating your responsibilities."

Daniel heard Rafe sigh. "It's a straightforward case, Daniel. We have a mountain of credible evidence to prove that Tony Taylor arranged Quentin Fisher's death. I shared most of the details with you the other day."

"But you don't have a credible motive for murder. Tony doesn't benefit from Quentin Fisher's death, nor does killing Fisher benefit the church. Just the opposite is true. Fisher's death broke the chain that leads back to McKinley Investments. The church is building a malpractice case against McKinley Investments, but we're working in the dark without Quentin Fisher."

"And your point is?"

"You sing with Tony, Rafe. You know that he's smart enough to understand that killing Quentin Fisher would hurt the church's chance of recovering its money."

"Most of the killers I've run into over the years were smart people who did stupid things. Intelligence gets pushed aside when emotions like hate take over."

"Do you really think that Tony Taylor is a murderer?"

Rafe sighed again. "Look, I don't like having Tony in jail any more than you do. If I had a single scrap of evidence that cast doubt on Tony's guilt, I'd do anything to prove he's innocent."

"I'll see if I can find that scrap for you."

"Stop right there, Daniel! I didn't invite you to play detective."

"No, but Tony did. He didn't kill Quentin Fisher. I intend to do my best to see that Tony is exonerated."

Lori parked the blue rental car on Oliver Street just west of King Street, a location that gave her a perfect view of Glory Community Church, and waited to see if her plan would work. If luck was still with her this noon, Ann Trask would go off for lunch, leaving Daniel Hartman alone inside the church building. It would be better— *much* better—to meet with the pastor without the chilling presence of the church's administrative secretary.

She glanced to her right. Sitting next to her on the passenger seat were the outside photos she'd taken of Glory's stained-glass windows, fresh from the inkjet photo printer at Glory Print and Copy Center. The fifteen pictures were excellent. They should be! She'd spent nearly four hours cropping, filtering and retouching them. Daniel would believe without question that she was a travel photographer in the making.

A flash of motion in the distance caught Lori's eye. *Ann Trask. Walking quickly toward the heart of Glory along King Street.*

Lori realized that she was holding her breath. She blew the stale air from her lungs and wondered why she'd begun to feel nervous. This was Glory, North Carolina, and Daniel Hartman was a pussycat—the easiest target she'd chosen during her three years of working for Chicago Financial Insurance.

Lori scooped up the prints and slipped out of her car. She had to act quickly; perhaps Daniel also planned to leave the building for lunch. She half walked, half jogged to the church's front entrance on Oliver Street. She trotted up the steps and made for the pastor's office.

She tapped on the frosted-glass square in Daniel's door. "Come in," was the somewhat puzzled, curt response.

Daniel had a plastic food container open on his desk and a half-eaten sandwich in his right hand. He looked up as she entered the office. "Miss Dorsett? Good morning—or is it afternoon?"

Lori flashed what she hoped was a radiantly ditzy smile. "You remembered my name. I'm flattered."

Daniel rose to his feet. "Have I forgotten an appointment?"

"No. I'm so excited about my photographs, I thought I'd drop in and show them to you.

He seemed momentarily confused. "Photographs? Oh, you mean the pictures you took of our windows."

Lori nodded as enthusiastically as she could. "I have a dozen photos to show you, except…"

"Except?"

"You're eating lunch. I don't want to disturb you."

"Have you had lunch?"

"No. I've been working all morning. I guess I forgot about eating."

"Your photos must be good."

"I want you to be the judge." She pushed the stack

of photos closer to Daniel and turned up her smile to full intensity.

"Tell you what…" he said. "Share my lunch with me before I look at the photos. I have two egg salad sandwiches. You take one."

"Half a sandwich is more than enough."

"With a glass of iced tea?"

"That would be lovely."

A new twinge of unease zipped through her. Daniel was acting the perfect gentleman and she planned to take advantage of his courtesy. Oh, well. It was her job to fool people. She had become expert at it.

"I'll be back in an instant," he said. "The kitchen is at the end of the hall."

Lori switched her smile to hyperdrive. "I'll be waiting."

No need to hurry. I have lots to keep me busy.

The electronic bug she'd brought with her looked like a squat gray cylinder not much larger than a bottle cap. She retrieved it from her purse and tore off the piece of slick paper that protected the layer of adhesive applied to its bottom.

She quickly surveyed the room and decided that the best location to mount the bug was beneath Daniel's overhanging desktop, close to his telephone. It would "hear" everything he said to people in the room and capture his half of telephone conversations. There was also little chance that the bug would be discovered: few cleaning people dusted the underside of a desktop. Lori pressed the bug into place against the wood surface.

Piece of cake.

The bug had a relatively short range, one hundred feet, at most. That meant she would have to hide a combination receiver/audio recorder in the bushes beneath Daniel's office window. It increased the risk of discovery, but there was no other easy way to surveil the pastor.

Lori took several calming breaths, stood and began to survey Daniel's office. One could learn a lot about a person from his everyday surroundings.

The furniture itself—old, heavy and made of cherry-wood—probably belonged to the church. It included a big desk, a credenza and two tall bookcases with glass-paneled doors. Three upholstered wing-backed chairs occupied the corners of the room and two smaller visitor chairs stood in front of the desk. The office, especially his desk, was lightly cluttered—a sign that Daniel was both busy and well-organized.

He had made the office his own by filling it with memorabilia of his years as an Army chaplain. There were photos of him in a desert setting that must be Kuwait or Iraq, and others of him teaching in a classroom. There were plastic models of military vehicles, including both a Jeep and a Humvee. And there were several items of religious paraphernalia that he used when preaching in the field, including a simple cross mounted atop a stand and a portable communion set.

Most impressive of all were two framed Purple Heart medals. Lori had known that Daniel had been wounded in combat, but seeing the actual medals made those injuries truly real to her.

This man is for real.

Lori dropped back into her chair. A few minutes later Daniel arrived with an empty paper plate, a plastic jug full of tea and a tall glass. He put half a sandwich on the plate and filled the glass. "There you go!" he said. "North

Carolina sweet tea—at its finest. However, I won't vouch for the egg salad—I made it myself."

Lori touched the plate, but then pulled her hand back.

"Is something wrong?" he asked.

"Do we have to, um…say a prayer or something?"

"I always pray before I eat. Would you like me to say a simple prayer for both of us?"

"Okay."

"The simplest grace I know is, 'Thank You Lord for the food we are about to receive.'"

"Amen!" Lori mumbled, hoping that Daniel would presume that this was a difficult moment for her.

She lifted the glass and sipped. The tea was sweet and strong, and with a hint of lemon. "Delicious."

She took a bite of the sandwich. The egg salad was nothing special and the bread tasted stale. "Yum! This hits the spot."

Daniel's hazel eyes shimmered. His face seemed even more handsome than usual.

Whoops. You're forgetting why you're here.

Lori pushed the collection of photographs closer to Daniel.

He picked them up. "So these are the shots you took when you visited us the other day." He slowly browsed through the pictures. "I'm impressed!" he said. "These are really good. You're a fine photographer."

"Thank you. I'm hoping that the inside shots will be even better."

"Well, I've never seen better photos of our windows."

"Pick the one you like best. I'll get it enlarged and framed. Consider it my gift for all your kindness."

"That's exceptionally generous of you."

Lori gestured toward the wall. "There's a perfect spot for a photograph a few feet past your diplomas and medals."

He laughed.

She went on. "Speaking of medals, I don't think I've ever met someone with two Purple Hearts. Where did you earn them?"

"Panama and Iraq. Happily, they were both minor injuries." An expression of surprise crossed his face. "You know, most people I know can't recognize a Purple Heart."

Lori bit her tongue. Your average ditz might not even recognize the image of George Washington on the front of the heart-shaped medal. She had made a tactical mistake. Now she would have to tell another lie.

"My dad had one," she said. "He fought in Vietnam. A piece of shrapnel hit his left leg."

"I see." Daniel paused, apparently to gather his thoughts. "May I ask you a question that might sound impertinent, Lori?"

"Sure. But I may refuse to answer it."

"Fair enough. When we first met, you mentioned that you no longer think of yourself as a Christian. May I ask why?"

Lori wiggled in her seat and tried to look nervous. This was the exact question she'd hoped he would ask— the question that would help to build their relationship. She had worked out an answer the night before, a simple answer that included lots of truth about her.

"I ran into a mixture of bad preaching, bad teaching and a church that didn't care at all about teenagers. I lost interest, stopped going to worship services and never looked back."

"Do you believe in God?"

Lori shrugged. "I'm confident He's up there some-where, doing His thing. But we've struck a deal. I leave Him alone and He stays out of my way."

"One day you might want God to take center stage in your life."

"Somehow I doubt that." Lori could tell that Daniel was holding back. He clearly wanted to say more about the joys of Christianity, but had decided to wait until another time. *Perfect.* She finished the half sandwich and drank the rest of her tea.

"Did you choose a picture?" she said abruptly.

"Ah—for my wall." He held up a print. "I chose this one. The window illustrates the well-known scene in the parable of the Prodigal Son when the delighted father runs out to meet his returning wayward offspring."

Lori took the print and put a small checkmark on the back. She glanced at Daniel. His wistful expression proved that her strategy had worked: he wanted to see her again. Now was the time to leave.

"I'm sure we both have lots to do this afternoon, so I'll say goodbye." She stood and reached across his desk. He rose and took her hand—at the same instant as Daniel's door swung open and Christine Stanton breezed into the room.

"Ooops!" Christine said. "I didn't know that you had a visitor, Daniel."

"I was just leaving," Lori said to Christine. She turned to Daniel. "The photo should be ready tomorrow." She eased her fingers out of his grip. "Shall I drop it off?"

Lori watched his face brighten. "Oh, yes, please do." Daniel seemed suitably pleased at the idea of seeing her again, tomorrow. *Double perfect.*

Lori nodded to Christine, who had begun to eye her suspiciously, and walked out the office.

"Phase One accomplished," she murmured as she breezed out of the building. "You're almost mine, Reverend Hartman, even though you don't know it yet."

FIVE

"What did she want?"

Daniel heard Christine's question loud and clear, but his mind stayed focused on the sound of Lori's footsteps as she walked along the polished hardwood floor in the church hallway.

"She wanted to see me, Christine," he said.

Without thinking about it, Daniel moved to his window and watched Lori climb into her rental car. He quickly realized that he was ogling more than watching—ogling at the way her skirt ruffled at the hem and how her attractive legs seemed to taper to a pair of high-heeled shoes that made her long legs look even shapelier.

Senior pastors of my age shouldn't ogle women.

He turned from the window to face Christine, whose eyebrows now arched precipitously.

"It goes without saying—" she spat out the words "—that Lori Dorsett came here to see you. My question, Daniel, was, what did she *want?*"

"Not much, actually. Lori...uh, Miss Dorsett wanted to show me the photographs she took of Glory Commu-

nity's stained-glass windows from outside the church.
She's quite proud of them—with good reason. They are
fine pictures."

Daniel tried not to frown as Christine made a harrum-
phing noise. What was going on inside her head to cause
this odd behavior?

When Christine said nothing in response, he went on.
"Miss Dorsett has promised to give me—uh, the church,
one of the photographs she took as a gift. It was nice of
her to offer, don't you think?"

"*Nice* doesn't begin to convey what I think."

There it was again—a sarcastic sharpness to Christine's voice. She seemed to ooze with irritation.

"You sound as if you don't like Miss Dorsett."

Christine heaved her shoulders. "I don't know her well
enough to dislike her."

"But something about her obviously bothers you."

"I'm beginning to think that Lori Dorsett is…is not
what she claims to be."

He perched on the edge of his desk. "You're saying
she's an imposter?"

Christine lifted her hands in a gesture that Daniel inter-
preted as a signal of uncertainty. "I don't know *what* she
is—and that's my problem."

Daniel wondered what he had missed about Lori that
had made Christine so upset. "Go on."

"Sometimes she's a ditz, other times she's bright
enough to use a complex camera like a pro. She's obviously intelligent and has a good vocabulary, yet when she
arrived at The Scottish Captain she came across like a
flaky airhead. She says she's newly divorced, but she has
more confidence around men than any recent divorcée

I've known. Even her flashy clothing doesn't seem right."
Christine jutted her chin at him. "Does any of what I'm
saying make sense to you?"

Daniel took Christine's hand. "I understand your
concerns, but I can't say that I have the same opinion. The
Lori Dorsett I just spoke to didn't strike me as flaky or
especially difficult to fathom. I think the shifts of behavior
you've observed are symptoms of her confusion as she
recovers from her divorce. I've seen it before in other
women. She's been through a shattering experience and
is trying hard to get back on her feet."

Christine sighed. "I guess we'll have to agree to
disagree. I intend to keep my eye on Lori Dorsett."

Daniel swallowed a chuckle. He'd enjoy doing the
very same thing. "Moving right along…" Daniel pointed
at a visitor's chair. "I'm all yours."

Christine remained standing. "I came by to give you
the latest news. Opposing counsel notified me that
McKinley Investments has found evidence that Quentin
Fisher warned George Ingles not to buy junk bonds. It's
only a monthly report that Fisher submitted—but an arbitrator could decide to believe it."

"George insists that Fisher never urged caution, that he
encouraged the church to make a risky investment."

She offered a wry smile. "One of them is lying. It
happens a lot when large sums of money are involved."

Daniel moved behind his desk as Christine marched
out of the office. She seemed in fine fettle, more joyful
now than when she'd arrived.

I wish I could say that.

He sat heavily in his chair, making the swivel mechan-
ism clang. How, he wondered, had Glory Community

Church managed to attract so much lying, deceit, suspicion, doubt and gloom?

He glanced at his calendar and was distressed to see that he had no scheduled appointments that afternoon.

This is not a day to be alone with my thoughts.

Daniel stood and moved to the window. It was a pity that Lori Dorsett had to leave. He would have enjoyed spending more time with her. What else could he do today?

You can start keeping your promise to Tony Taylor. You need to do more than make telephone calls to the police.

"I know," he murmured. "I'll visit the scene of the crime."

Daniel scribbled a note to leave on Ann Trask's desk:

> My cell phone is turned on if anyone needs to reach me. Just between you and me, I'll be at the Glory at Sea Marina on Water Street.

Daniel climbed the outside wooden stairway to the business office that sat above the Glory at Sea Marina's chandlery and ships' store. He stopped for a moment to take in the view. The marina's five long piers were laid out parallel to each other like the tines on a plastic pick comb. More than a hundred boats—some sail, some power—were docked in the slips between the many short-finger piers that were attached perpendicularly to the main piers.

The breeze was fairly stiff, at least fifteen knots, which raised whitecaps on the water and worked together with the bright sun to make the Albemarle Sound sparkle like a bowl full of blue jewels. The air was clear enough for Daniel to make out two lines of red and green buoys that extended into the Sound. They marked the marina's narrow entrance channel. Seagulls swooped beyond the channel and a small motor cruiser equipped for fishing bobbed on the choppy surface.

How Tony must miss this view.

Daniel abruptly pictured Tony Taylor sitting alone in a dingy jail cell in Elizabeth City. He put the thought out of his mind and turned the knob to open the door.

He saw Rebecca Taylor sitting at Tony's desk, talking on the telephone. She covered the receiver with her hand and whispered, "I'm almost finished with this call, Daniel."

He stood by the door while she talked. What did he hope to accomplish today? His snap decision to "visit the scene of the crime" was prompted by the detective novels he'd read and the TV cop shows he'd watched.

You don't have any idea of what you're doing.

"True enough," he murmured. "I have to trust God to show me the way."

Rebecca hung up the phone, came around her desk and gave Daniel a big hug. "Oh, my, am I'm happy to see a sensible person. Most of the boat owners think that Tony killed that evil man and should be given a commendation. I keep trying to explain that Tony didn't kill anyone—but no one believes me." She concluded, with a pleading look in her eyes, "Except you, of course, Daniel."

Daniel made a noncommittal grunt. What could he say to Rebecca? *Let's hope you're correct.* He desperately wanted Tony to be innocent. But every discussion with Rafe Neilson spawned a fresh crop of doubts. What if Tony really had killed Quentin Fisher? Daniel decided to keep any negative thoughts to himself. It would be too easy to get into a destructive argument with Rebecca Taylor.

She stood a head shorter than her husband, but had a

commanding presence that made her seem his physical equal when they were together. Daniel knew that she'd turned fifty in January, because he'd helped Tony arrange a surprise party for her. Rebecca told her friends that she was a "true redhead—a gal with golden-brown eyes, pale skin, lots of freckles and a furious temper." She was the chief nurse at Glory Regional Hospital and was well known for her ironlike determination and drive.

No. Only a fool gets into an argument with Rebecca Taylor.

She linked arms with Daniel and asked, "To what do I owe the pleasure of this visit?"

"I'm sure that Tony told you what he asked of me."

She nodded. "He needs to know that there are people in his corner who actually care about him."

"I understand how he feels." Daniel let his smile fade. "Naturally, I agreed to help, but I'm not sure how. I know so little about what happened."

"*No one* knows what really happened that afternoon. The police evaluated the so-called evidence they found and came up with a ridiculous conclusion."

Daniel willed himself to maintain a neutral expression. Rebecca was being unrealistic.

Why not? She loves Tony.

Daniel cleared his throat. "Where was *Marzipan* docked? That seems a good place to begin my education."

"Follow me."

Daniel followed Rebecca down the steps, across a parking lot and through a metal gate in the tall chain-link fence that protected the marina's five long docks.

"Our five docks are labeled A, B, C, D and E. Tony kept *Marzipan* there." She pointed at the first slip on E

Dock. "Tony selected the spot because the water is quite shallow—barely deep enough to keep *Marzipan* afloat. It's not an area of the marina that customers would willingly choose for their boats."

"I assume that's why the fire on *Marzipan* didn't spread to other boats. There were none docked nearby."

Rebecca shielded her eyes against the sun and looked at Daniel. "Tony's boat didn't simply catch fire—it blew itself to smithereens. Thankfully, the force of the explosion went straight up. And no—*I mean, yes*—the nearest boat was several slips away. Had God not been watching over us that day, the damage to the marina and the other boats could have been a lot worse."

"Did the explosion completely destroy *Marzipan*?"

"Well, most everything above the waterline is gone. The bottom of the hull survived—the cops lifted it out of the mud and trucked it away." Rebecca sniffed. "All Tony has left of *Marzipan* is a charred steering wheel—we found it lying on B Dock—and a lot of photographs taken of the boat during happier times."

"I've been told that Tony loved *Marzipan*."

She sniffed again. "Let's put it this way… I'd have never asked Tony to choose between *Marzipan* and me."

Daniel put his arm around her shoulder. "You'd win every time. I've seen the way Tony looks at you."

She chuckled. "Maybe…but the vote would be close."

"When this nightmare is over, and Tony comes home, he'll buy a *Marzipan II*."

"Not likely, Daniel. *Marzipan* was an antique that Tony rebuilt by hand. It was worth lots of money. Our insurance company rejected our claim because they accept the lie that Tony caused the explosion."

Daniel couldn't think of anything comforting to say. He merely shook his head sadly.

Rebecca went on. "The really weird thing is that the explosion happened during our busiest time of year— right when people get their boats ready for the sailing season. Tony had too much on his mind during those two weeks to worry about the church's money or Quentin Fisher." She added, "What else do you want to see?"

Daniel looked out over the marina. *Tell her the truth, you have no idea.*

"I've seen enough to get me started," he said.

Daniel felt awkward about his little fib, but he didn't want to admit to Rebecca that he hadn't a clue about what to do next. He began to wish that he'd never made such an impossible promise to Tony Taylor.

The strong breeze made walking pleasant, even though the sun had sent the afternoon temperatures into the high eighties. Daniel set off for Glory Community Church at a brisk pace. He turned onto Osborn Street and collided with Rex Grainger, a heavyset man in his early sixties, who was nearly as tall as Daniel.

"We now know what can happen," Rex said as he readjusted his eyeglasses, "when two men who are prone to contemplation go walking through Glory. I was mentally outlining my next editorial. Are you planning your next soporific sermon, perhaps?"

Daniel smiled at the gentle barb. Rex was a member of Glory Community Church. "Actually," Daniel said, "I was thinking about Tony Taylor."

"Now that is a coincidence. He'll be the subject of my next editorial."

"Maybe our chance meeting wasn't by chance? Have you ever seen the bumper sticker that reads, 'A coincidence is God's way of remaining anonymous'?"

Rex peered at Daniel. "I hope you're not going wonky on me, Reverend."

"I'm serious, Rex. I need information about Tony, and I can't think of anyone in Glory who's in a better position to give it to me. After all, you are the distinguished editor of our splendid newspaper." He added, "Where are you off to?"

"I was returning to our building on Osborn Street, but I'll be happy to follow you anywhere if you keep dishing out your over-the-top praise. It's so much nicer than the stack of whining letters to the editor that are waiting for me on my desk."

"No need to change your destination. I'm heading back to the church, your office is on the way."

"Lead on, Daniel—and tell me what you need to know."

"I'm afraid that's my main problem. I'm trying to understand the case, but I don't know what questions to ask."

"I see." Rex hesitated. "Yes, I do see! Tony's pastor definitely should have the latest skinny on the case."

·Daniel thought about correcting Rex's misreading of his interest, but that would require an explanation of his real purpose—an explanation that Daniel didn't want to give.

"I've browsed through the *Gazette*," Daniel said, "but I haven't found much about Tony Taylor in recent issues."

"That's because we're in a lull. Tony's trial is months away and the murder of Quentin Fisher is no longer front and center in people's minds."

"I cringe when I think about a trial. I can't stand the thought that Tony might be convicted."

"*Might* be convicted? The police and the prosecutor act like it's a slam-dunk case. A sure conviction! One of my sources says the evidence absolutely, positively, proves that Tony killed Fisher."

"Oh, my. Tony insists he's innocent."

"That's hardly news."

"I believe him."

Daniel watched Rex's eyebrows knit together. "Well, the NCSBI doesn't."

"The NC…what?"

"The North Carolina State Bureau of Investigation. That's the organization that retrieved the remains of Tony's boat. They took it off to a lab somewhere and figured out what caused the explosion."

"Are they competent?"

"The NCSBI? Of course they're competent." Rex squinted at Daniel. "You don't know much about state and local law enforcement, do you?"

Daniel shook his head. *And even less about being a detective.*

"Tell you what, Reverend—I'll put together a file of background information that will bring you up to speed on the details of the case."

"Bless you, Rex." Daniel truly meant it.

Stop smiling at me! Lori wanted to shout. No matter where she had gone that afternoon to take pictures, people had waved and kibitzed and smiled endlessly. The citizens of Glory were certainly trying to prove that they lived in the friendliest small town in North Carolina.

But every smile—every friendly nod—added to her growing sense of distress. She felt uncomfortable deceiving these gracious folks who went out of their way to be hospitable to a stranger. Kevin had been right. She found it increasingly difficult to remind herself that the end justified the means—that her job was to root out any lies.

Lori had taken to the streets of Glory to bolster her cover story. A fledgling travel photographer wouldn't spend all her time shooting the stained-glass windows at a rather ordinary church. Lori had to be seen out and around, poking her lens at other photogenic subjects. She'd captured images of five different statues, several charming gardens, the decorative stonework on the Glory National Bank building and a large goldfish that its owner deemed a Koi.

She'd also taken a minute to place the surveillance receiver/audio recorder in a rhododendron bush a few feet away from Daniel's window. Kevin Pomeroy called the black-plastic gadget a "Magic Box"—it was smart enough to ignore most random noises and zero in on human voices.

A Magic Box that had the look and feel of an MP3 audio player, complete with a small display screen and a headphone jack. Anyone who discovered it lying below the bush would assume that the device was dead and had been discarded. Only Lori could bring it to life—by inserting an electronic key into a slot on the edge. Lori had two Magic Boxes with her—one for each of the electronic bugs she carried.

Lori wondered what she should do with all the pictures when her assignment was finished. Papering the walls in Kevin Pomeroy's office was a definite possibility. Or maybe she would send them to the person most responsible for the afternoon's photo session: Christine Stanton.

Christine's glare when she saw Lori in Daniel's office had expressed confusion, displeasure, warning and, most of all, suspicion.

"Face it," Lori muttered. "Christine has elected herself Daniel's protector and she's worried that a 'ditzy divorcée' is about to sink her claws into him."

Christine's distrust would complicate the task of getting close to Daniel, but…

But I don't have any other candidates. Daniel is it.

It was essential that Christine—and the other townfolk—continue to believe her cover. And so Lori had invested four hours of her time to take useless digital photos under the hot North Carolina sun. She felt ready to call it a day by 5:00 p.m. and looked forward to a quick shower and another nice place to eat dinner.

"Hello, Lori—we meet again."

Lori spun around—into another of Christine Stanton's expressions. This one conveyed civility, calmness and a touch of resolve. How, Lori wondered, had Christine managed to stumble across her in front of the Baptist church on Osborn Street?

Because she went looking for you, that's how. Good thing you decided to take pictures.

"You startled me, Christine," Lori said.

"Oh, I doubt you scare that easily."

Lori heard a thick vein of satire in Christine's tone.

I'll play your game, counselor. Let's fence some more.

"What are you doing on this side of town?" Lori asked.

"I walk three miles every day. What brings you here?"

"Photography, of course."

"Photography…" Christine peered at the church. "Does First Baptist have interesting windows, too?"

"Not really—but the landscaping is spectacular. Definitely worth photographing." She made a sweeping gesture toward the beds of shrubbery that enclosed the building. "Don't you agree?"

Christine ignored Lori's question. "What are your plans this evening?"

"Nothing special. After I clean up, I'll try a new restaurant. The Fisherman's Inn was delightful—do you have any other suggestions for dinner?"

"Yep. Join me in my apartment on the third floor of the Captain. I made a tray of lasagna this morning. My aunt's recipe is famous on two continents, but it serves eight people. I need help eating it."

Lori hoped that the surprise she felt didn't show on her face. Christine had decided to act on her suspicions. *She* was maneuvering to get closer to the curious newcomer.

Lori considered the invitation. Spending quality time with Christine could be chancy. Christine's hospitality was clearly driven by her curiosity. Dinner would be a time of interrogation and probing.

And yet, visiting the woman's apartment would offer a perfect opportunity to plant the second surveillance bug that currently resided in the false bottom of the black leather camera case.

It's an easy decision. You have to take the risk.

"I *love* lasagna. Thank you for asking." Lori pointed to her rental parked at the curb. "I have my car. Can I give you a ride back to the Captain?"

Christine shook her head. "I love to walk before dinner—it's the only chance I have all day to think." She added. "Shall we say six-thirty?"

Lori willed herself to beam at Christine. "I can't wait."

* * *

At 6:40 p.m., Lori climbed the private staircase in the
rear of The Scottish Captain that led to the third-floor
apartment. Dithery dilettantes never arrive on time. She
had chosen her clothing carefully: a clean pair of cotton
slacks, a blouse that was too dressy for a private dinner
and pumps with heels a tad too high. She knocked gently
on Christine's door.

"Come in," Christine called. "The door's not locked."

Lori knew that she'd blinked in amazement. For a
moment she imagined she'd entered an antique shop, or
perhaps a living museum that featured a late nineteenth-
century home. The large parlor featured plum-colored
wallpaper, overstuffed upholstered sofas and chairs, dark
and well-polished wooden furniture.

"I'm in the kitchen tossing our salad," Christine called.

Lori walked through the parlor into a small but thoroughly modern, kitchen—all off-white and stainless steel.
The only wood in the room were a pair of cutting boards
on the granite countertops and a compact round dinette
set that could sit four.

"It's lovely up here," she said.

"This apartment is one of the perks of my job as
night manager."

"Ah." Lori nodded.

"Emma Neilson finally finished refurbishing the apartment just before she married Rafe. Everything in the
kitchen and bathroom is brand-new. The parlor is furnished with bits and pieces borrowed from throughout the
house. And the bedroom—you can see for yourself. It's
the middle door that leads off the parlor."

Lori dutifully followed Christine's instructions. Her

bedroom faced Broad Street and seemed light and airy. Its furniture dated to the 1950s: simple lines, plastic trim, conical legs and light-colored wood, probably maple.

"The bedroom furniture came from a thrift shop, didn't it?" Lori said when she returned to the kitchen.

"Every last square inch of Formica surface." Christine laughed. "Living here requires one to be mental gymnast. I'm never sure what year I'm living in." She laughed again. "But the price is right, so I can't complain." She gestured with her chin toward a pitcher on the dinette table. "Pour yourself some iced tea."

Lori sat and filled a glass.

Christine came to the table with a tossed salad and a breadbasket full of dinner rolls. "I've wanted to ask you something for the past two days. How come you chose Glory to photograph? We're not well known as a travel destination—yet."

Lori quickly gathered her thoughts. Liars needed to have good memories—hers was one of the best.

"I suppose that I found Glory more or less by accident. My mentor back at the Chicago Institute of Graphic Arts suggested ten different parts of the country that would be good locations for practicing my photographic skills."

Lori tried to look sheepish. "I discovered that the Albemarle region was the cheapest of the ten—the price of lodging seemed especially reasonable. I'd spent so much money on my camera system that I had to start economizing."

"Your mentor? Is he a photographer I'd have heard of?"

"*She*. Her name is Molly Clawson. She's fantastic, but I don't know if her fame reached the east coast."

Lori sipped her ice tea. When Christine called the Institute in Chicago—as she undoubtedly would—she'd learn that Molly Clawson was away on a sabbatical and that, yes, Lori Dorsett completed the certificate program in travel photography the previous December.

Christine would receive this information from Francine Pomeroy, the school's assistant dean, the executive assigned to answer all inquiries from the public. Francine was the wife of Kevin Pomeroy.

Lori continued. "Once I chose the Albemarle region, I began reading brochures and Web sites. I fell in love with Glory from a distance. The rest, as they say, is history, if you'll forgive the pun."

"Indeed." Christine leaned across the dinette table. "So…what do you think of Daniel Hartman?"

Lori had been expecting the question, but it still sent a shiver up her spine. She began with a suitably ditzy answer. "I've never heard him preach, but he seems like an excellent pastor."

Christine nodded. "He's an excellent pastor. But I'm more interested in how you see Daniel as a man."

"He strikes me as a good man. One who believes in his calling. He has an ability to put people at ease. I'm sure he's excellent at tending the flock—or whatever it is that pastors do."

Lori could almost feel Christine's growing frustration. "All of what you say is true," Christine said evenly. "Daniel is a good man. In fact, many single women in town are intrigued that he never married. He's considered one of Glory's most eligible bachelors."

"Really?" Lori worked hard to sound bewildered. "I could never marry a pastor. They don't make enough money." She gave a little shrug. "My ex-husband often called me a high-overhead wife—I suppose it's true."

A buzzer sounded.

"The lasagna is ready," Christine said, her tone considerably cooler than before. "I'll be right back."

Lori had put her handbag, the top unzipped, close to her right foot. She quietly dropped her right hand to her side then let her fingers slide into the handbag. They quickly located the little round bug. Lori had already removed the slick paper from the adhesive.

Lori had decided to attach the bug to the underside of the dinette table as soon as she entered the kitchen and noted the three file boxes stacked in the corner. There was a compact fax machine sitting on a nearby countertop and, propped against the wall, a thick black attaché case that was just the right size to hold a laptop computer.

Lori felt sure that the kitchen served double duty as Christine's office and that she used the dinette table as a makeshift desk.

Lori pressed the little bug under the tabletop, about a foot from the edge, a location where it couldn't easily be seen. A moment later Christine arrived with a large baking dish full of sizzling lasagna.

"It looks fabulous," Lori said.

"Sure…but it's the *taste* that that will bring you back for seconds and thirds." Christine peered at Lori. "Do you mind if I say a simple prayer before we eat?"

"Not at all."

Christine reached across the table and took Lori's hand.

"Heavenly Father, we thank You for the food we're about to eat and the fellowship among friends we're enjoying this evening. In Jesus' name we pray. Amen."

Lori added a soft, "Amen," amused that Christine could shift mental gears from suspicious interrogator to spiritual "friend" by merely closing her eyes. That had been true of so many of the so-called Christians Lori had met when she was young: pious while praying, cutthroat the rest of the time.

How had her mother described people who honored Christian principles in every aspect of their lives? *Salt and Light.* That was it.

Lori unfolded her napkin. She hadn't been fooled by Christine Stanton, not a bit. She was a tough, suspicious woman who would do anything in her power—right or wrong—to ensure that the church got its money back.

I'm going to enjoy stopping you. But tonight, I'll eat a big helping of your superb lasagna.

SIX

Lori awoke on Thursday morning with a start. Something was wrong. It took a few seconds for her mind to register that the sunlight streaming into the room seemed too bright. She glanced at her alarm clock. Nine o'clock. *Nine?* Had she slept through the alarm, which had been set for six-thirty?

No. You forgot to set your silly clock.

After dinner, the evening before, Christine Stanton had invited her to watch a favorite DVD from her collection: *The Verdict*, a classic legal thriller from 1982 that starred Paul Newman. Lori had no reason to refuse, so she hadn't returned to her room until nearly eleven. Then she'd spent almost an hour finding the right place to hide the Magic Box that would receive the signals from the bug she'd planted underneath Christine's dinette table.

The Magic Box had to be out of sight yet also be located as close to the bug as possible. Lori finally decided to place the gadget inside her spare purse—a smallish cloth bag—and set the bag on top of an occasional table near the front door. If Lori had guessed right, the bug was almost directly overhead.

It had been midnight when Lori climbed into bed—and neglected to turn on her travel alarm clock.

Lori slipped out of bed. Breakfast was served at the Captain between seven and nine-thirty. Lori wasn't especially hungry—not after two helpings of Christine's magnificent lasagna—but she did want a cup of coffee and a glass of juice.

She dressed quickly, gave her hair a few brush strokes, then trotted downstairs.

Emma smiled at her. "You slept late today."

"Right through a ringing alarm," Lori fibbed.

"That's a good sign. Our slower Southern pace is finally overwhelming your high-stress, big-city lifestyle." She offered Lori a menu. "Are you ready for breakfast? Our chef outdid himself this morning. Baked petite pancakes filled with sliced hardboiled eggs, bacon and melted Swiss cheese, drenched with homemade Hollandaise sauce."

"Goodness! I wasn't going to eat breakfast."

"That sounds like Chicago talk. Are you in a hurry this morning?"

Lori shook her head. "Not really. Maybe I'll nibble on one pancake."

"*Nobody* can eat just one." Emma pointed toward the breakfast room. "Take a seat—I'll be right back with your coffee."

Lori didn't even try to argue.

Lori returned to her room feeling exceedingly full and carrying a mug of coffee. She remembered to look inside her cloth purse. A tiny light glowed red in the corner of the Magic Box. Lori felt a rush of adrenaline. She plugged her access key into the slot.

The little display screen read, "Recording 1—8:38 to 8:44 a.m."

You should have checked before you went downstairs!

Lori connected an ear bud to the Magic Box and pressed the play button.

"Hey, Daniel, it's Christine." Lori adjusted the tiny earphone to lock into her left ear and began to relax. The bug had captured Christine's side of the conversation perfectly.

A few seconds of silence, then, "Great. I hope you're doing well, too."

More silence.

"Uh-huh. Well, I just received a conciliatory fax from McKinley Investment's attorney. I'm inclined to believe the firm wants to settle the case before it gets to binding arbitration."

A longer silence.

"I think so, too. It's the best news we can hope for. You, I and George need to meet this morning so I can bring you both up to date."

A short pause.

"You pick the time. My preference is that we meet sooner than later."

An even shorter pause.

"Ten o'clock is fine with me. I'll call George after you hang up. See you later."

Lori heard several soft clicks—the sounds of Christine dialing another number.

"Good morning, George. It's Christine."

A brief silence.

"Early, my foot. The sun has been up for more than two hours."

A longer pause.

"In any case, we need you over at the church at nine-thirty."

A few seconds of silence.

"True, but you have nearly an hour and fifteen minutes to shower, shave and get to Daniel's office."

A very short pause.

"Suck it up, George, and look on the bright side. Life is difficult—but it may soon get a lot easier."

Click.

"What a jerk!" Christine muttered.

The Magic Box went silent.

Lori glanced at her watch. Nine fifty-nine. The meeting of the Big Three would start in one minute. How did she want to handle it? She could let the Magic Box under the rhododendron do its thing. Or she could plug her earpiece into the gadget and listen to the conversation as it took place.

It's sounds like too interesting a meeting to wait.

Lori treaded softly down the stairs and slipped out of The Scottish Captain without attracting Emma's attention. Two minutes later she parked on Oliver Street, across from the entrance to Glory Community's parking lot. She approached the church via a looping path so that no one looking out of Daniel's window would see her.

The Magic Box was where she'd place it. When she picked it up, her heart skipped a beat. *No red glowing light.*

The device hadn't recorded *anything* since she'd hidden the bug beneath Daniel's desk. But that made no sense. A busy pastor would have had several conversations in his office and who knew how many phone calls. Either the bug or the Magic Box had failed.

She jammed the little device into her purse, her mind

racing to find a solution. She didn't have the remote sound monitor with her or the tripod to hold it. Worse, she had already missed two or three minutes of conversation. The meeting might be over by the time she traveled back to the Captain for her gear, drove back and set everything up.

You have to switch to Plan B.

Lori exhaled slowly. Eavesdropping in person was always risky, but she had no other choice.

She entered the building and tiptoed toward Daniel's office. The door was open and Christine was saying, "I expected to receive a feeler from McKinley Investment, but not quite so early."

Lori moved back from the door and observed her surroundings. Where could she plant herself where she wouldn't be seen?

Of course! The church library. The alcove adjacent to Daniel's office had been lined with bookshelves. If she stood next to the shelf that backed up to Daniel's wall she might be able to hear people talking. Better yet, the books gave her an excuse for being there. If anyone saw her, she could pretend she was looking for a book.

Not a great scheme, but better than nothing.

She took up position close to the shelf.

"I made copies of the fax for both of you," Christine said. "It's obvious that McKinley Investments is looking for a way out of arbitration. They don't want Quentin Fisher's misdeeds to become public knowledge—that won't do their squeaky-clean image any good. They also want to limit the risks they face."

Daniel's office fell silent. The Big Three must have been reading the fax.

"Yes," Daniel finally said. "I agree with your interpretation. The fax mentions 'an amicable compromise that will satisfy both parties.' What do you suppose that means?"

George dove in. "That's lawyer-speak for 'we don't want to give back all the money you lost because of Quentin Fisher.'" He added, "They want us to settle for less."

Christine responded. "Of course they hope that we'll settle for less, George. It's called *compromise.* That's what happens when both parties work together to end a lawsuit."

"If we do compromise," Daniel said, "how much money will we leave on the table?"

"Well, if I had to guess, I'd say that a fair settlement would be to recover sixty percent of our total investment."

"You mean we lose nearly *four hundred thousand dollars?*" George shouted.

"I'll remind you again, George," Christine said evenly, "we're talking about a *compromise,* an agreement that both sides accept, but which neither side likes. A sixty percent settlement means that we'll get back more than half of the money we invested, while McKinley Investments has to shell out six hundred thousand dollars." She took a deep breath. "Keep in mind McKinley Investments will have to dip into profits to pay us. They're not happy to do that."

"Half a loaf is not good enough," George said, his voice much more shrill. "I vote we see it through and recover all of our money."

Lori heard a chair scrape, then three footsteps, then crockery clinking. She guessed that Christine had stood and moved to the side table to refill her coffee cup. "If we 'see it through,' to use your words, George," Christine said, "we have no guarantee of winning at arbitration. We might lose everything. An amicable settlement will at least return a big chunk of money. Sixty percent is a lot better than zero."

"I don't agree with you," George said. "There's an important moral dimension to this case. We were taken in by Quentin Fisher. He perpetrated fraud on us when he recommended those risky investments to the church."

"Please be careful with your language, George. Fraud is a *crime*. We haven't alleged that McKinley Investments is a den of thieves. Our claim argues that Quentin Fisher failed in his duty to recommend sensible investments for the church. That's negligence, not fraud."

"Quentin Fisher is a cheat! I know a lot about junk bonds. Six years ago, before I retired, I even co-wrote an article about junk bonds for a financial magazine."

"You're joking?" Lori could clearly hear the shock in Christine's voice through the plastered wall.

George seemed to misread Christine's distress. "Nope. I'm serious. *HR Finance* is more of a journal than a magazine, but it's well known among human resource professionals. You may be able to Google the article on the Internet."

"George, that's the very last thing I'd want to do!" Christine said loudly. "We need to keep your article our little secret. Is that understood?"

"Why?" The voice was Daniel's.

Christine sighed. "Because if George's old article establishes that our financial secretary has expertise with junk bonds, we can hardly claim that the church was taken in by Quentin Fisher's bad advice."

"I see," Daniel said. "We lose our primary argument."

"Along with our case," Christine said gloomily.

"That doesn't make much sense to me," George said.

"Perhaps not," Christine said, "but I know what I'm talking about."

"Indeed you do," Lori murmured to herself.

Thank you, George, for sharing.

Lori heard more chair shuffling followed by George's voice. "Guys—I promised Margo that we'd go to Norfolk, Virginia, today. We were supposed to leave at nine-thirty. If I don't get home soon, Margo will fricassee me."

"On your way, George," Christine said. "Norfolk's gain is our loss."

Lori snickered. She wondered if George had detected the sarcasm in Christine's farewell. A moment later George's heavy footsteps tramped down the hallway. He walked past the alcove without noticing Lori.

One down.

Lori looked around the library. Should she try to sked-addle out of the church without being seen or stay put until Christine left Daniel's office?

"I'd best be going, too," Christine said.

Lori moved closer to the bookcase. The decision to stay had been made for her. With luck, Christine wouldn't spot her either.

"Before you leave," Daniel said. "I have a…*concern*."

"Let me guess," Christine responded. "Is it wrong and/or unethical to suppress George's article?"

"Exactly. I don't want our claims to be based on a lie."

"They aren't. We've asserted that Quentin Fisher took advantage of George's lack of knowledge. The mere fact that George co-wrote an article doesn't change anything. I hate to say this, but we both know that George Ingles is a blowhard who pretends he's a financial whiz but who actually knows very little. *That's* the truth, Daniel."

"I'll think on it."

"You do that."

Lori heard a curious shuffling sound, then realized that Christine had hugged Daniel.

Lori stood absolutely still as Christine walked determinedly down the hallway without looking to her left or right.

Two down.

Lori began to tiptoe away, but then made a U-turn in the hallway. There's no more need for stealth, she thought. Why not make this visit wholly legitimate by saying hello to Daniel Hartman? She knocked on the frame of Daniel's open door.

"Lori? What brings you here today?"

"A book," she said quickly, astonished by the intensity of his smile. He was definitely beaming at her.

She went on. "I mean that I'm looking for a book… well, not necessarily a *book*…a brochure will do fine…uh, I need *anything* that explains the history of your windows."

"I have a pamphlet about the windows somewhere among my papers."

"May I borrow it?"

"I'll make a copy for you." Daniel stood and moved from behind his desk. "This is really a remarkable coincidence, Lori."

"It is?"

"I'd planned to call you this morning."

"You did?"

He nodded, then said, "Would you like to have lunch with me today?"

"More food?" Lori said before she could stop herself.

"As a matter of fact, yes. There's a delightful restaurant in town you probably haven't been to yet—the Glorious Table."

Lori cranked up her smile to match Daniel's. If she wasn't careful, she'd gain twenty pounds on this assignment.

"I'd love to have lunch with you."

Daniel took a step toward her. "The Glorious Table is a beautiful old building at the corner of King Street and Stuart Lane."

"I know where that is."

"Shall we meet out front at twelve-thirty?

"It's a date."

Lori watched Daniel go red. An instant later she felt herself blush.

Lori's high spirits were abruptly dampened by a chill that seemed to split her in two. She realized that she'd just agreed to a "date" with a man that she was about to betray. Moreover, her assignment in Glory would end the instant she'd gathered sufficient evidence to demolish the church's case against McKinley Investments. George Ingles's financial article might be enough all by itself.

She stepped backward through the doorframe before Daniel could move closer to her.

"I have an errand to run." Her voice had become throaty. "I'll meet you at twelve-thirty."

She trotted down the hallway, eager to get outside and use her satellite phone to call Kevin Pomeroy. She had to tell him what she'd learned about George Ingles.

Unless I do it quickly, I won't want to do it at all.

Daniel decided that Glory Community Church felt tranquil in a way that only an empty church building can achieve—still and holy, with a faint odor of furniture polish hanging in the air. But now he could also detect Lori Dorsett's perfume, a soft and lovely scent, with a hint of flowers.

Even a pretty woman is not enough to stop me brooding about George Ingles.

Christine had described George perfectly: a blowhard who knew less than he claimed about finance.

Daniel dropped into his chair. The meeting with Christine and George had been a trial. Through it all, he'd wanted to shout at George, "If you were half as smart as you think you are, you wouldn't have lost nearly a million dollars of the church's money. And don't forget Tony Taylor. He's in jail, charged with murder, because of your dumb dealings with Quentin Fisher."

Don't forget to yell at yourself, too.

Daniel's years in the military had taught him that a commander was responsible for the mistakes made by the soldiers in his unit. It was a lame excuse to say that the church had relied on George and that he had let everyone down.

Daniel slapped his palm against the top of his desk. The pastor of Glory Community Church should have paid more attention to what George had been doing.

I should have done a better job watching over the church's money.

Daniel rocked back in his chair and gazed at the wall. His office could use a fresh coat of paint, but probably wouldn't get one this year—thanks to George Ingles.

He suddenly felt a need for prayer—for discernment, for patience, for trust, most of all for forgiveness. *God, I have a long list of requests today, but I know You're up to the job.* He closed his eyes tried to empty his mind of all evil thoughts.

Daniel was delighted that Lori arrived at the Glorious Table the same time he did, a full five minutes early. There was nothing ditzy about her punctuality, or the speed at which she'd accomplished a complete change of outfit. Since he'd last seen her, she'd replaced her faded blue jeans and checked shirt with tan slacks, a yellowish blouse and light blue blazer. She'd knotted a small silk scarf around her neck and propped her sunglasses on top of her head.

He thought the overall effect stunning. Lori Dorsett had to be the prettiest woman in Glory.

"Hello, Lori."

"Hello, Daniel."

"I predict that you'll enjoy this place. It's my favorite restaurant in Glory."

She looked around the first-floor dining room. "Well, I certainly love the yellow-and-red decor. And I've never seen so many photos and paintings of Scotsmen in kilts."

"This is the one restaurant in town that really pays homage to Glory's Scottish heritage. Some people don't like the Scottish motif. They think these stern-faced Scotsmen make the place look too masculine and military."

Lori moved close to Daniel. "It's not too masculine or military for me." She smiled; the room abruptly seemed brighter to him.

Daniel wondered if any of his parishioners were lunching in the Glorious Table. What would they think if they saw him with Lori at his side? Probably not much. The folks in town were beginning to think of Daniel as a confirmed bachelor.

Everyone would assume that you've hired her to take pictures of the church.

He cast a sideways glance at Lori as she stood comfortably beside him. For some reason he wanted to keep looking at her. Had he ever gone out with a woman as striking? Probably not.

If anyone asks about "your type" in a woman, you now have an answer.

Daniel asked the hostess for a table that overlooked the building's back garden. They were seated at a spacious corner table that provided a grand view of a long line of spring-blooming rosebushes in reds and yellows and pinks.

Daniel noted a frown flash across Lori's brow when she studied her menu. He realized that she was concerned about the restaurant's high prices. How, he wondered, would she handle the situation?

"Do you have any recommendations?" she said. "I'm leaning toward the Isle of Skye Chicken Salad."

Daniel concealed a chuckle. The Table's chicken salad, deservedly famous throughout North Carolina, was also one of the lowest priced items on the menu. Lori had given him an opportunity to signal how expensive a lunch to order.

"The chicken salad is superb, but I've been dreaming about the Mary Queen of Scots Tournedos all morning."

Signal delivered, Daniel thought. The tournedos luncheon was the most expensive meal on the menu. Lori now knew that she could order anything in between.

This woman is not a ditz.

Daniel decided to make his dream come true when the

waiter returned to take their order. He wasn't surprised when Lori followed her initial meal inclination.

She lifted her glass of iced tea for a toast. "Thank you for your invitation. I've been eating alone since Sunday. This is a pleasant change."

"I feel the same way."

"Really? You have an unhappy look on your face, as if you'd rather be somewhere else. It's mostly in your eyes."

"Now you know why I never play poker. What you see on my face is leftover misery from this morning." He sighed. "Lunch with you is a bright spot in an otherwise gloomy day."

"Do you want to tell me about it?"

"Why would I want to burden you?"

"Because I'm a good listener. Because it helps to talk these things out. Because I'm a friendly stranger who'll be gone in a few days, so you can say things to me you might not want to say to your close friends and colleagues."

Daniel laughed. "Okay. I take your point." He slid a basket full of bread sticks to the center of the table. "Let me know if I begin to bore you."

She grinned. "Count on it!"

"The church received a large gift last year, nearly a million dollars. But it's gone, every last cent, because the church made a series of poor investment decisions."

"Wow."

"Wow and a half. I almost wish that John Caruthers hadn't left us so much money. His gift almost split the church in two during the past two years. Worst of all, it was the motive for murder."

Lori nodded slowly. "I recall hearing something about that the other day, but I don't remember who told me."

"It could've been anybody." Daniel shrugged. "The whole town lived through the mess with us."

"I just remembered. The gentleman I met the other day in your office who said he was the financial secretary."

Daniel nodded slowly. "George Ingles." Daniel felt like telling Lori the whole sordid story, but that wouldn't be fair to George.

Lori stared into her glass of iced tea. "Perhaps the church is better off having lost the money?"

"That might have been true last year, but early this year the Elders decided to spend the lion's share of the money to support music missions throughout North Carolina. Two dozen less fortunate churches are counting on us. We'll have to dip into our operating budget to keep some of the promises we made."

Daniel glanced at Lori. The encouraging expression on her face had been replaced by a look of dismay. "You never announced that Glory Community intended to use the money for mission work," she said.

"We didn't want lots of publicity, but we planned to give away almost seventy-five percent of the total."

"Then why did your financial sec…uh, I mean the church make risky investments?"

"You guessed right—the poor investments we made were incredibly risky. The idea was to make our nest egg larger. The more money we had, the more poor churches we could help."

"I had no idea you intended to give so much money away."

Daniel reached across the table and patted Lori's hand.

"Thank you for being concerned, but it really is our problem. With God's help, we'll muddle through."

"Almost a million dollars…" she said softly.

"I don't think we've lost the full amount."

She peered at him. "Really?"

"I suppose I can tell you something in confidence. You are a 'friendly stranger,' after all. We've made a claim against the investment firm that led us astray. We believe they want to settle with us. We may get as much as sixty percent of our money back."

Daniel watched Lori's expression change again. Her eyebrows drew together in dismay as she looked off into space. Her eyes seemed to glisten. Had he said anything that would make her cry?

Good work, Pastor. You certainly know how to show a lovely woman a happy time.

enough to show my mentor that I've become a competent travel photographer."

Lori watched Daniel's shoulders sag and his expression droop. His lively hazel eyes lost much of their sparkle. The weight of the world seemed to settle on him.

"I see." He nodded slowly. "Of course, you haven't accomplished one of your goals. You didn't take pictures of our stained-glass windows from the inside."

"That's true. Perhaps I'll have the chance before I leave."

"And when will that be?"

"Saturday morning, I suppose. That will give me plenty of time to make flight reservations and pack up all my gear."

"Last-minute airline tickets are expensive. Why not wait a few days—save yourself a bundle of money."

Lori thought quickly. She couldn't tell Daniel that the price of airline tickets was the least of her worries. "I can standby for a flight at no additional cost."

Daniel grinned. "Well, Saturday morning gives the populace of Glory more than twenty-four hours to get you to change your mind."

Lori had a new thought. Glory Community Church would take years to recover from the permanent loss of its mission money. The pastor would have an especially tough time of it. That's why Daniel looked as though the weight of the world had settled on him. *It had.* A good man like Daniel Hartman deserved a better future than that.

She suddenly found it difficult to look him in the eye.

Lori turned west on Main Street and tromped on the accelerator. She didn't want to go back to The Scottish Captain, she didn't want to take any more pictures of

Glory, and most of all she didn't want to think. Perhaps a drive in the country would help.

She reached Glory's town limits; Main Street became State Route 34A. Lori knew that the two-lane road followed a bow-shaped path that had a big westward bulge and eventually reached Elizabeth City, twenty miles away. The flat terrain wasn't especially pretty, mostly marshland and stands of pine trees, but it seemed to take her mind off Daniel Hartman.

What else could you have done? You work for Chicago Financial Insurance; they pay your salary.

Lori slowed the car so that two large crows pecking at a dead raccoon on the road could flap out of her way.

"You could have thought about the consequences more carefully before you surveilled the church," she murmured.

A new thought popped into her mind. *Maybe you can un-notify the company about George Ingles?*

Lori saw a service station up ahead. She parked the car next to the food mart and found the satellite phone in her handbag. She climbed out of the car and dialed Kevin.

"Hello, Mizz Dorsett, I've got great news for—"

Lori interrupted him. "Kevin, what I told you earlier is probably not the whole truth." She spoke loudly and quickly. "The more I think about the circumstances of this case, the more I'm certain that Quentin Fisher took advantage of George Ingles. He probably played George's ego like a violin. On paper, George looks like an expert. In reality, he's a retired executive trying to keep everyone's respect by pretending to be a financial guru."

"Whoa! Slow down. What's this all about?"

"I don't want you to tell anyone else about George Ingles's financial article."

"That horse has been out of the barn for more than an hour, Lori. That's my great news. After you called earlier, I immediately ordered a deep search in the Lexis/Nexis database. It took ten minutes to corroborate everything you said. George Ingles co-authored an article about the use of speculative equities in employee investment plans. I have a copy of the article sitting on my desk. I sent another copy to McKinley Investments' lawyers—with a note explaining that my ace investigator uncovered it.

"The article is surprisingly well written and informative. Based on that document alone, George would be considered knowledgeable about junk bonds. We also found another publication that explains how George participated in a task force on the subject. We have everything we need to prove that neither the man nor church was duped. End of story."

"It's not over for me. Quentin Fisher could have sold George Ingles the Eiffel Tower with a little bit of flattery."

"So what? All we need to prove is that George is a junk bond guru. That's an almost ironclad defense to the claim that McKinley Investments in general—and Quentin Fisher in particular—led the church astray."

"I'm not happy about this."

"You should be jumping for joy. The church won't collect from McKinley Investments and Chicago Financial Insurance Company won't have any liability. The case will be closed in a few days. Justice has triumphed—the good guys have won." He continued, "You do great work!"

"Do I really?" Lori could hear the unhappiness on her own voice. "I don't feel like an effective worker right now."

Kevin groaned. "That's because you've identified with the bad guys. I told you the other day, it happens on every assignment you handle."

"The people at Glory community church aren't 'bad guys,' Kevin. They're some of the nicest folks I've met in years. I think the case should go to arbitration. Let an arbitrator decide if the church is right or wrong."

Another, louder groan. "Stop thinking about that church and start imagining what you'll do with the spectacular bonus I intend to give you this year. I see a fire-engine-red new convertible with your name on the registration."

"I don't want to feel sleazy every time I drive it."

"Lori, you dropped the dime on George Ingles by bringing *facts* to light. You didn't lie or fabricate evidence. You didn't load the deck against him. Ingles really, truly, qualifies as an expert on junk bonds."

"But the only reason we know that is because I fooled three nice people."

"Take a few days off, Mizz Dorsett. Go to the beach. Go shopping. Forget about Glory, North Carolina."

Lori hung up. She wasn't in the mood for the beach. She didn't want to go shopping. She didn't feel like driving aimlessly anymore. And she was tired of talking to Kevin Pomeroy. She switched the satellite phone from Standby to Off.

She slid into the rental car and drove back to Glory. Christine was puttering around in the Captain's side garden when Lori pulled into the parking area. Lori returned her wave—and her smile.

"More picture-taking?" Christine said.

"Nope. I did a bit of reconnoitering," Lori fibbed, "checking out sites for the future." She continued to walk as she spoke. This wasn't the occasion for a sociable chat with Christine. A wrong word, carelessly spoken, might trigger Christine's lawyerly curiosity and give the game away. She would find out soon enough about the true target of Lori's surveillance activities.

"I'll see you later," Lori said with a wave.

"Sure thing."

Lori sighed. She had told yet another fib. In fact, she would do her best to avoid Christine Stanton until it was time to check out of The Scottish Captain on Saturday.

My time of making friends in Glory is over.

Praise God! Blue skies and gentle breezes!

Daniel let the slat on his Venetian blind snap back into place. He couldn't ask for a better day for sailing a small boat.

He felt well. He'd slept well for the first night in months. And why not? He was about to enjoy a short break from this miserable financial business.

The idea of inviting Lori to go sailing came to him just as he was drifting off the night before. A junket on Albemarle Sound would make her last day in Glory memorable. And because he enjoyed her company, a half day on the water would be a mini-vacation for him.

First things first. He reached for the telephone and dialed Dave Early at his gas station on Queen Street.

"Hello Dave, it's Dan Hartman."

"Howdy, Pastor." A pause. "Is anything wrong with your car?"

"Nope. I'm calling because I'd like to borrow your sailboat today—uh, that is if you're not using it."

"Right! I'll shut down the garage and go sailing on a perfectly good workday." Daniel heard a snorting noise that he assumed was laughter. "You may borrow *Anticipation* for as long as you'd like today. She's sitting in slip B6 at the Glory at Sea Marina, undoubtedly feeling neglected."

"Is she ready to go?"

"Pretty much. Her fuel tank is full of diesel, the water tank probably needs to be topped up." Dave laughed. "Feel free to varnish her topside, teak and wax her decks, if the spirit moves you."

"Thanks, Dave. I owe you one."

Daniel next dialed The Scottish Captain. Emma Neilson answered the phone.

"Hi, Daniel. Your name doesn't show up very often on our Caller ID. What can I do for you?"

"I'd like to chat with Miss Dorsett."

"O-k-ay." Emma, her voice dripping with surprise, managed to add two extra syllables to the word. "I'll put you right through."

The phone rang four times, making Daniel worried that Lori might not be in her room. On the fifth ring, she answered.

"Hello? This is Lori Dorsett."

Lori's straightforward greeting conjured up an image of her smiling face in Daniel's mind. He leaned against the edge of his desk and enjoyed the almost electric tingle that seemed to accompany his thoughts about her.

"Lori, it's Dan Hartman. I want to see you again."

"You do? When?"

"Today. Let's go sailing."

"You mean in a *boat?*"

"A pretty twenty-seven-footer named *Anticipation.*"

"Well…"

"You'll be able take some great photos of Glory from out on Albemarle Sound."

"But…"

Daniel kept talking. "I know it's your last day in town, so let's make it a good one."

"Do you have the time to take me sailing? Shouldn't you be…uh, working on your sermon, or doing something else ministerial, if that's the right word?"

"Funny you should say that. Friday is usually my sermon preparation day. Ann Trask doesn't schedule any appointments for Friday. She won't try to reach me unless there's a congregational emergency. However…"

"However?"

"I awoke at dawn's early light this morning and finished my message. I can play hooky this afternoon with a clear conscience. We both know that I need some time away from my office—and I want to spend it with you."

"Well…"

"You said that that already. I'll pick you up at ten o'clock. The forecasters say it will be a perfect day, with an afternoon temperature in the low eighties."

No answer.

Daniel broke the silence. "I'll have you back at the Captain no later than four. You'll have plenty of time to pack."

"Oh, boy."

"Why are you hesitating?"

"The truth is that I feel…*guilty*."

"Don't be! My sermon is finished and I have nothing else on my calendar. Cross my heart." He paused, then said, "Say you'll come with me."

Daniel heard Lori exhale heavily. "I give up. I'll meet you outside the Captain at ten."

He felt like cheering, but settled for saying, "I drive a silver sedan."

* * *

Daniel gently pulled the tiller. *Anticipation* turned a few degrees to the left; the sails caught the breeze and the Catalina 27 accelerated.

"Shall we make another run?" he asked Lori.

"Nope. I've taken every photograph of Glory I can think of, using most of my lenses and filters."

"Then we'll head out into Albemarle Sound and have lunch."

He smiled at Lori, who sat opposite him in the cockpit. She was wearing a pair of white cotton shorts and a blue-and-white polo shirt. She looked surprisingly nautical—and even prettier than she had the day before.

"So…what do you think?" he said.

"The day is everything you said it would be. I'm having a lovely time. Thank you for being so persistent."

Daniel mentally recited a silent prayer of thanksgiving—and apology. He'd encouraged Lori to come sailing without asking if she was prone to seasickness. It was a foolish thing to do. Over the years, Daniel had cut short many a sailing afternoon when a guest had turned green.

Happily, Lori had proved a wholly competent sailor. She scampered around the boat with the sure-footedness of an experienced seafarer, helping him trim lines and shifting her weight when necessary.

"I can tell that you've been sailing before," he said.

"Don't forget that Chicago is on Lake Michigan," she replied. "I learned to sail when I was a kid."

When she returns to Chicago, Daniel thought, she'll go sailing with other men. He felt a nasty clutching sensation inside his chest—and recognized it as simple jealousy, an emotion he hadn't experienced in years.

Daniel changed the topic. "Are you flying home tomorrow?"

"Yes. But not until five in the afternoon. I don't have to go standby. I'm booked on a direct flight from Norfolk."

"Lots of people in Glory will be sorry to see you leave. You've made many friends in town."

"Have I?"

"Without doubt."

"Well, maybe." Her eyebrows flickered; she seemed bemused.

"I know what you're thinking. 'It takes time to get to know people.'" He tapped the top of her hand. "That's because you're used to living in a big city, where nothing is quite as it seems. Glory is a much simpler place. People aren't devious. If they act like they like you, you can believe it. What you see is what you get."

Lori didn't say anything in reply. Her expression verged on the uncomfortable.

"A penny for your thoughts," Daniel said.

Lori was about to say something, then seemed to change her mind. She shrugged and gazed at the shore.

"Now I'm really curious. What has made you look so pensive?"

She turned back slowly to face Daniel, then sighed. "I wonder if anything is ever as it seems."

"None of that! You're much too young to be pessimistic. Especially when the sky is clear and the sun is shining. This is a day for optimism." He added, "Speaking of sunshine, I believe you need another coating of sunscreen. Your arms are turning red."

He gestured toward the cooler in the front of the cockpit. "While you're doing that, I'll switch on the autopilot and break out lunch. We have two Super SOGgy Heroes from Snacks of Glory."

"*Two?* One of those monsters is enough to feed a family of five."

"When you go to sea, take ample provisions—that's my motto."

Lori laughed. Daniel found it difficult to take his eyes off her. For the past three hours Daniel had felt as excited as a teenager on his first date. His only distress during their "date" had come during their walk through the Glory at Sea Marina. Rebecca Taylor had seen him with Lori. The look on her face seemed to ask, Why was Daniel going out for a sail with a beautiful first mate when Tony was languishing in jail?

And, shouldn't Daniel be spending all his spare time trying to prove Tony's innocence?

Daniel had felt a frisson of embarrassment, but not because of Lori. *Be reasonable, Rebecca—it doesn't make any difference what the pastor does with his spare time because he doesn't have a clue how to conduct a murder investigation.*

Daniel knew that the autopilot attached to the tiller would hold the boat on a specific compass course. He could leave it in charge of the helm as long as the wind didn't change direction. Daniel would have to keep his eye on the *Anticipation*'s wind vane as they ate. He rummaged through the cooler and brought out one sandwich, which he cut in two.

"Can I ask you a spiritual question while we eat lunch?" he said.

"Let me guess. Why haven't I felt like a Christian since I was fourteen years old?"

"That's it! I've been curious since you talked about it the other day. What happened to turn you away from the church?"

"What happened…" Lori echoed. She abruptly frowned. "You won't be surprised to hear that not all pastors are as nice as you and not all Christians are as nice the folks I've met in Glory."

"Ah. You were hurt by a church."

"Ripped to shreds and thrown away—by a pastor and several church leaders who went out of their way to crucify my mother."

Daniel held his breath.

Lori grimaced. "I suppose you want me to tell you what happened?"

"Only if you are comfortable doing so."

She ate for a while without speaking. "My dad died when I was twelve," she finally said. "About a year later the choir director turned his attentions to my mother. They eventually developed a thing for each other." Her expression froze. "The trouble was, he was married and had three young kids."

"When did their relationship stop being a secret?"

"When one of the choir members saw them together."

"Ah."

"The choir director blamed my mother for 'leading him on,' and everyone in the church believed him. A hundred 'good Christians' came to the crazy conclusion that my mother wanted to remarry and was willing to break up a happy marriage to find herself a new husband."

Lori sniffed. "Fourteen is a tough age to see your mother driven out of a fellowship that she loved."

Daniel could see that Lori had never forgiven her mother's tormentors, which meant that the healing process had never started within her. Perhaps he could help Lori begin to heal?

Not when she lives in Chicago and you live in Glory, North Carolina.

Daniel spoke softly. "The church blamed your mother, and you blamed God."

"I guess I did." Lori stared into space. "Where was God when she needed Him? Why did He let such a terrible thing happen to my mother?"

"God never abandoned her, Lori. He was with your mother amid her worse trials—He's with you today."

"Well, it sure looked to me like He took off for parts unknown. In the end, we had to move to a different neighborhood in Chicago."

"How did your mother feel?"

Lori stared at the deck. "I was afraid you'd ask me that. My mother never lost her faith. In fact, she insisted that God helped her get through the really tough times."

"But you still feel differently."

"Uh-huh. I think God ignored her prayers. She didn't deserve what happened to her."

"Have you ever chatted with God about your feelings?"

"Is that a suggestion that I start praying?"

"No. I said *chat*. Tell God how you feel, then listen quietly for His answer. He may surprise you by having a good one."

Daniel knew better than to press the matter much further. He paused to finish his sandwich, then said, "I understand how you feel, Lori. Lots of believers go through dry spells when God seems far away. That's because God isn't pushy. He'll let you ignore Him until

you figure out the truth. Which is really a good thing."
He smiled at her. "My prayer is that, in the fullness of
time, you come to appreciate that God has always been
part of your life. You may even discover that you haven't
really stopped being a Christian."

"I'll think about it. I promise." She began to chuckle.

"What strikes you as funny?" Daniel asked.

"Remember what I said earlier—things aren't always
as they seem. I was speaking about bad things that seem
good, but I suppose that there can also be good things
that seem bad."

"That's an interesting observation. I should do a
sermon on the topic."

"You told me your sermon was finished," she said with
mock concern.

"A *future* sermon." He checked her paper plate. Empty.
"Do you want half of the second sandwich?"

"Nope. I want to steer the boat."

Daniel unhooked the autopilot. Lori slipped into the
helmsman's seat and took hold of the wooden tiller that
moved the boat's rudder. He saw himself partially reflected in the brown-tinted lenses of her sunglasses.

"Where would you like to go?" she asked.

"You choose—you're in control."

She grinned at him, and with that grin Daniel knew that
his world would never be the quite the same again. The
Reverend Doctor Daniel Hartman, Minister of Word and
Sacrament, had fallen in love with Lori Dorsett.

EIGHT

Lori touched the Page Down key. Another photo of the Glory Strand flashed on her laptop screen.

"That's the last shot I put in the photo display program," Lori said. "I've taken hundreds more photographs, but they're all duplicates of the pictures you've seen."

"They're extraordinary," Emma Neilson said. "I'm impressed. Thank you for showing your collection to me."

"Thank you for asking to see my work," Lori replied.

"Speaking for myself, I think it's a pity that you finished your school assignment so quickly. I hate to see you leave Glory." Emma smiled. "I know that there are other people in town who feel the same way."

Lori returned Emma's smile. News travels quickly in a small town. Her two "dates" with Daniel Hartman had probably launched a flood of tittle-tattle. They'd made no attempt to keep their activities a secret.

Poor Daniel. Wait until the unhappy news gets out.

In a few days the normal process of legal discovery would reveal to Christine Stanton that McKinley Investments knew all about George Ingles's "little secret." Christine was smart enough to figure out Lori's role in uncovering the all-important article that George wrote. By then, Lori would be long gone.

Would people in Glory get mad at her for doing her job? Probably so—but that was their problem, not hers. As Kevin had wisely pointed out, she hadn't lied or invented evidence. All she'd done was uncover the truth and make it known to Chicago Financial Insurance.

How would Daniel react? she wondered. Would he feel especially awkward because of their dates? Well, she hadn't wanted to have dinner with him or to go sailing. He'd pushed hard to get her to agree.

True, she enjoyed herself on both occasions. True, Daniel Hartman was exceptionally pleasant to be with. True, she experienced the occasional "warm and fuzzy" feeling for Daniel—but then, he was a good-looking man and it had been months since she had been on a real date.

All that would change when she returned to Chicago. She'd been working too hard, going on too many business trips. It was high time to put some effort into building a better social life.

And instead of buying a new car, she would use a chunk of her promised bonus money to take a real vacation. Today's sail was delightful. Perhaps a Caribbean cruise would be fun? Or should she charter a sailboat in the Mediterranean?

A tap on her arm brought Lori back to the present.

"What are you going to do with your photographs?" Emma asked.

Lori could feel a perplexed expression sweep across her face. *What would happen to the pictures?* They were part of her "work product." She would turn the digital files over to Kevin Pomeroy when she got back to Chicago. He would probably bury them in a database somewhere.

Except for a few souvenirs I intend to hang on to.

Lori switched the laptop to Standby. She would definitely keep the shots she took of Daniel Hartman captaining the sailboat on Albemarle Sound.

"I don't have a good answer for you," Lori said. "I'll show the pictures to my mentor, but after that, I really don't know what will happen to them."

"You might consider offering them for sale to the Glory Chamber of Commerce."

"Really?"

"You've captured the essential charm of Glory. I don't know of a better series of current photographs. I'd love to include a few in my brochure."

"Well, thank you for the suggestion." Lori bit her tongue. Kevin would probably fall over laughing when she shared this conversation with him.

Emma continued. "Your pictures are fresh and exciting. I predict a productive career as a travel photographer for you. I wish you best of luck."

Emma surprised Lori by giving her a big hug.

Lori surveyed her clothing and gear laid out across the bed and wondered why repacking to go home always seemed harder than packing to leave home. She hadn't bought any clothing or souvenirs in Glory; nonetheless her belongings seemed more voluminous for her suitcase.

First things first.

Lori began by stowing the expensive surveillance gear safely in the bottom of her camera case. "What should I do about the two bugs?" she murmured.

Leave them where they are, that's what.

Lori coiled a power cord around her hand. Kevin would be annoyed to lose the two pricey bugs. But she had no convenient way to get into Christine's apartment or Daniel's office on Saturday morning. Even asking to visit these locations could cast suspicion on herself. That was last thing she wanted to do on her last day in town.

Sorry Kevin. I suppose that our bonuses will be a bit smaller this year.

"It's bad planning to schedule all your onerous chores for Saturday morning." Daniel grumbled as he carried his plastic laundry basket down the creaky wooden staircase that led to the manse basement.

Particularly this Saturday morning, he thought. He might be able to see Lori Dorsett once more before she left. He intended to call her at nine, possibly even offer to buy her breakfast.

He tugged the pull cord that turned on the single overhead bulb and hoped that any curious insects would skitter away, making it unnecessary for him to tromp on them.

Let's say that you manage to see Lori, then what?

Had he ever felt this way about a woman before? Perhaps years earlier—but never in Glory. Okay, but what was he going to do about his feelings?

In a few hours Lori Dorsett would leave North Carolina, maybe never to return. He had signed on as pastor at Glory Community Church "for the duration," as he liked to joke. That meant he was committed to living in Glory for at least another decade. A woman in Illinois plus a man in North Carolina didn't add up to a successful relationship.

Daniel heard "Amazing Grace" chiming somewhere above his head and realized that his cell phone, sitting upstairs on his kitchen counter, was playing its "church business" melody. Because only a few people rated that unusual "ring," it was probably an important call. He abandoned his socks and underwear atop the washer, climbed upstairs two steps at a time, and flipped open the phone.

"Dan Hartman."

"It's Christine, Pastor. You, George and I need to meet. At nine o'clock. Today."

Daniel decided that it made no sense to ask Christine if a hastily arranged Saturday meeting was essential—she wouldn't be calling at 8:10 a.m. on a lark.

"Our usual place?"

"No!" There was a definite growl in her voice. "I definitely don't want to meet at the church. Drive to the Albemarle Diner, out on State Route 34A. I'll buy you breakfast."

"You sound mad, Christine."

"I'm rip-roaring steamed. You'll learn the reason why at nine."

Daniel hung up and reviewed the to-do list affixed to his refrigerator with a cross-shaped magnet. He could gas up his car on the way to the meeting and get a haircut another day. His pantry, though, needed a serious restock. He couldn't put off a trip to the supermarket much longer. Yesterday, he had run out of coffee, milk and eggs.

Let's see what today brings.

Fifty minutes later he parked alongside Christine's green convertible. The Albemarle Diner had been built the previous year, but looked like a leftover from the 1950s— an architectural anthology of stainless steel, glass and neon lights. The diner served famously delicious waffles.

I can withstand the temptation. All I need for breakfast this morning is a bowl of cereal.

Daniel found Christine and George occupying an out-of-the-way booth near the back of the diner. He squeezed in next to George—and noticed that his seat mate shot a nervous glance at Christine.

Something is seriously wrong.

"Good morning," Daniel said with a nod toward each of the others.

"We don't have any time to waste this morning, so I'll dive right in." Christine began to count on her fingers. "First, Daniel, I ordered a deluxe waffle breakfast for you—I know how much you like the waffles here. That's your large glass of orange juice and there's your mug of coffee.

"Second, we are meeting away from the church this morning to preclude any chance that a spy will overhear what we say. Third—"

"I beg your pardon, Christine," Daniel interrupted. "Please explain what you mean by a spy overhearing us."

"Hold your horses, Pastor. All will be clear if you let me finish." She resumed her count. "Third, I received a telephone call late last night from one of the senior partners at the law firm that represents McKinley Investments. He engaged in what we lawyers call 'back channel communications.' He told me, entirely off the record, that McKinley intends to defend against the church's lawsuit on the basis that George is an acknowledged expert on the subject of junk bonds."

"No!" Daniel said, more loudly than he meant to. A woman in the adjacent booth turned her head. Daniel smiled at her.

Christine went on. "When I asked my new friend

how McKinley had reached such an erroneous conclusion, he suggested that I have a talk with George about an article he co-authored for *HR Finance* about six years ago."

Daniel moaned, then said, "They seem to know everything."

"Indeed they do!" Christine emptied a packet of sweetener into her coffee. "The lawyer thought he was doing me a honking big favor by giving me a heads-up. He assumed that our leading witness hadn't told me the whole truth, and that I would feel like a horse's patootie when the information came out during the arbitration hearing."

"I wonder how they found out about the article," Daniel said.

Christine made a face. "Give me a break, Pastor! They found out because someone told them. We have a spy in our midst. A snitch. A mole." She peered at him. "Close your mouth, Daniel. You'll attract flies."

Daniel didn't want to ask his next question; he feared that he already knew the answer. "Do you have any idea who provided the information to the opposition lawyers?"

Christine rolled her eyes. "Isn't it obvious? Glory Community Church has been infiltrated by the lovely Ms. Lori Dorsett. She sold us down the proverbial river."

Daniel could hear his heart thumping. He wanted to argue with Christine but felt too stunned to respond. He drank some orange juice and was finally able to say, "How can you be sure that Lori is the culprit?"

Christine made a dismissive wave with the spoon she had just used to stir her coffee. "Think it through, Daniel." Christine began a new count, this time using her spoon as a pointer. "First, the woman showed up in

Glory a few days after I filed our lawsuit against McKinley Investments. That's kind of convenient, don't you think?

"Second, she gave us a cockamamie reason for choosing to visit Glory. We've got a pretty little town, but it's hardly a place that would encourage a fledgling travel photographer to travel a thousand miles.

"Third, out of all the bed-and-breakfasts in the area, she chooses The Scottish Captain. Do you suppose that could have something to do with my job as night manager?

"Fourth, on her first day in town, she decides to take pictures of the stained-glass windows in our obscure house of worship—the very same church that's suing McKinley Investments.

"And fifth, look who she makes friends with. None other than the pastor of the aforementioned church, who despite his excellent discernment in other matters takes the woman dining and boating."

Christine reached across the table and gripped Daniel's hand. "I hate to be the one to tell you this, my friend, but Lori Dorsett is a deceitful woman who has lied repeatedly to all of us."

Daniel stared at the hand that Christine held. It seemed almost disconnected from his body. "But why would she do such a thing?"

"Because she's some sort of private investigator. I don't know who she works for, but her bosses clearly have an interest in seeing that we don't win the case. As I see it, the three most likely contenders are McKinley Investments itself, their law firm and the liability insurance company that must be lurking somewhere in the background."

"Could there be another explanation?" Daniel asked.

"I don't want to be hasty in reaching a conclusion that will damage someone's reputation."

"I asked myself the same question, Daniel—but then I found these." Christine opened her hand and displayed two small cylindrical objects made of dull gray plastic.

Daniel stared at the cylinders for a few moments, then asked, "Are those what I think they are?"

Christine nodded. "Fairly high-quality electronic bugging devices. I found one underneath my kitchen table this morning. I raced over to the church, let myself in with my key and retrieved the second bug from under the rim of your desktop."

Daniel's tongue turned to cotton. He took another drink of his orange juice.

"Lori was sitting at my kitchen table while I poked around in my kitchen. I didn't pay any attention to what she was doing. She had ample opportunity to plant the bug." Her eyebrows arched as she asked, "Did you ever leave her alone in your office?"

Daniel nodded woodenly. "I went to the kitchen to get us both cups of coffee." He struggled to wrap his mind around the horror of Christine's conclusion. *Lord, don't let this be true.*

He poked at the bugs with his index finger. "What made you search for those infernal contraptions?"

"I get suspicious when my legal opponent learns about a major weakness in my case a few hours after I do." Christine's expression turned grim. "Planting electronic surveillance devices to capture our oral communications is a crime in North Carolina. I'm convinced that Lori Dorsett is responsible, but I don't have solid proof. If I can find relevant evidence, I'll go to the police and have her arrested."

Daniel winced. He didn't even want to contemplate another friend in jail. He had a sudden thought. "Aren't these devices listening to what we're saying right now?"

"Sure—but there's no receiver in range to pick up their signals. You need to be within a couple of hundred feet of bugs this small to capture voices. They have very low power transmitters." She added, "Over the years, I've received a practical education in surveillance techniques."

"God save us all," Daniel prayed softly.

"We're meeting here as a precaution. She may have planted more bugs in Glory that I haven't found. I didn't have an opportunity to search all the possible hiding spots in my kitchen and your office."

Christine dropped the two plastic-cased bugs into her handbag, then reached inside. "Oh, and one more thing. I bought three prepaid cell phones this morning. We'll use them whenever we have to talk about the case—in the event that the woman managed to tap our telephones. We don't want to reveal any more of our secrets to the opposition."

Daniel heard George groan softly beside him. "I feel so incredibly dumb," he said. "Not only am I responsible for the original loss of the church's money, I may have ruined our lawsuit with my foolish bravado in your office."

Daniel had heard a torrent of moaning and groaning from George in recent weeks, but this confession made Daniel feel genuinely sorry for the man. He clapped a hand on George's shoulder. "We had no way of knowing that Lori Dorsett was—" Daniel searched his mind for a nonjudgmental term "—not acting in our best interests. Don't blame yourself for trusting people."

"Exactly, George!" Christine said. "Fool me once, it's your fault—but fool me twice and it's mine. Her actions have taught us everything worth knowing about Lori Dorsett. From now on, we can take the appropriate precautions when dealing with her. Think of her as a rattlesnake or a sewer rat."

Daniel started to object, but thought better about it. He realized that he wanted to defend Lori—despite her outrageous behavior, despite the enormous damage that she apparently did to the church.

Falling in love does funny things to people.

"Ah!" Christine said. "Here comes breakfast. I'll say the blessing this morning."

Daniel found it impossible to focus on Christine's prayer. His mind had locked on a single thought.

I have to see Lori Dorsett.

Lori sat in the gazebo behind The Scottish Captain and willed the hands of her wristwatch to move faster. Her bags were packed, she'd paid the bill, but it made no sense to leave for Norfolk, Virginia, much before one o'clock and it was only ten-fifteen. Lori had considered hitting the road early and doing some sightseeing along the way, but she quickly rejected the idea. She didn't feel interested in playing tourist today.

Because you're waiting for Daniel to say goodbye.

Lori smiled even though no one was watching her. It was certainly true that she expected Daniel to drop by the Captain this morning. At the very least, he would probably ask for her address and telephone number in Chicago. Chances were, he'd never actually call her—but then again he might. Men are unpredictable that way.

She heard heavy footfalls on the narrow flagstone path that ran along the side of the bed-and-breakfast. She turned to see Daniel striding toward her, his face angry, his eyes livid. He spoke before she could begin to react.

"Who are you? What are you?" His voice was cold and harsh—and frighteningly commanding. "I want the truth."

Lori shuddered. *He knows.*

She took a deep breath and decided that another lie was not an option. "I'm not a travel photographer or a recent divorcée," she said softly. "I work as an investigator in the Loss Control Office at the Chicago Financial Insurance Company. We'd be the ones writing the check if McKinley Investments is ordered to return the church's money."

Daniel nodded. "Christine guessed as much." His eyes darted hither and yon, seemingly looking at everything in the Captain's back garden except her face. He climbed the short flight of steps the led into the gazebo and glanced at the bench. But instead of sitting next to Lori, he leaned against the railing.

"I don't understand how you operate," he said. "Does that mean you were sent to Glory to make sure that we didn't get our money back?"

"No, I was sent here to learn the truth." She smiled at Daniel. "Seek diligently to discover the truth, deterred neither by fear nor prejudice."

His expression signaled his puzzlement. "I've heard that line before."

"I'll bet you have." She chuckled. "Here's another slogan that should sound familiar. 'Do what has to be done.'"

"That's the CID motto." He peered at her, his eyes piercingly alert. "Are you retired Army?"

She stood to attention and delivered a crisp military salute. "Warrant Officer Special Agent Lori Dorsett,

U.S. Army Criminal Investigation Division reporting for duty, Sir."

"Oh, my…" He added, "You're a professional."

"I like to think so. I'm good at what I do."

Lori regretted her words the instant she spoke them. Daniel frowned. "Lying, cheating, deception, illegal surveillance—have I left anything out? Oh, yes, photography. Where did you learn to take pictures? I presume that you really didn't attend the Chicago Institute of Graphic Arts."

"The Army taught me to take pictures. I've been certified in forensic photography. Of course, shooting photos of buildings rather than bodies is a novelty for me."

"Is *anything* you told me true?"

"It depends. My cover is fabricated, but most of the personal details I shared are true."

"Did the Army also teach you the fine points of electronic surveillance?"

"Surprisingly, no. I learned most of what I know from my current employer."

"Christine found two bugs—are there any more scattered around Glory?"

"No."

"Good! She wants to press charges against you, but doesn't think that she has enough evidence."

"She doesn't. Those bugs have a special surface that won't retain fingerprints. For all we know, they were planted by leprechauns."

"I see." He hesitated, as if he were gathering his thoughts. "That leaves one item to explore. *Us*." He looked away and asked, "Was I merely a surveillance target? I want to know."

Lori was beginning to feel numb. But since he wanted

to know, why not tell him? "You started out as my target and then graduated into a friend."

"I graduated?" Daniel blinked twice.

Lori sighed. "You asked for the truth, Daniel. I've given it to you. I came here to do a job. You may not think it's a nice job, but insurance fraud is a fact of life—even in perfect little towns like Glory." She moved a step closer to him. "At first, I saw you as a source of information. But then, when I got to know you…"

"No!" Daniel bellowed. "This is absurd! We're holding what seems like a normal conversation, but everything you've done is inexcusable. You can't justify your lying and deception with hand-waving explanations. It's morally wrong to seek the truth with lies. Don't you get it?"

"Do you think it's better to leave the truth hidden?"

"What is your concept of truth? Sure, George wrote his silly article, but it's equally true that he didn't have enough financial smarts to see through Quentin Fisher's dishonesty." Daniel took a deep breath. "Your success may have delivered a fatal blow to our church. If that was your goal, congratulations!"

"I don't want to hurt the church, Daniel, or you."

"Go back to Chicago. Glory is too small a town, too unsophisticated, for the likes of you."

She watched Daniel leave the back garden, his head shaking as he walked. He looked a beaten man as he retraced his way along the flagstone path to the front of the Captain.

She thought about calling after him—about urging him to come back—but why bother? He would never, ever, forgive her for…for doing what had to be done.

We live in two different worlds.

Lori sat on the bench. "It's better this way," she murmured. "Much better."

No. It's not better.

The abrupt thought raced through her mind. She shivered as an icy feeling of despair encased her heart and filled her body. She had driven Daniel Hartman away. For keeps. Forever.

Lori looked at her hands, tightly clasped in her lap.

Please God. I don't want him to go.

Lori gasped. She realized that for the first time in more than twenty years, she'd said a prayer.

It felt…strange, but nice.

NINE

Daniel felt he was running on empty. He'd almost reached the point of not caring about the church's lost money. Or about the surveillance bugs. Or about the new round of legal maneuvers that Christine Stanton insisted on talking about in a second meeting she scheduled for twelve-thirty that Saturday afternoon.

At least the meeting was in Daniel's office. She had searched the various nooks and crannies and pronounced the room "clean."

Daniel had cheerfully volunteered to sit in a visitor's chair when she asked to occupy the chair behind the desk. She had covered its twelve square feet of surface with legal and financial documents.

The complete history of Glory Community Church's relationship to McKinley Investments lay splayed across the polished cherrywood desktop. The mood in his office had never been darker. All he could do to improve the situation was to pray.

Today that didn't seem enough.

Daniel glanced at George slumped in the other visitor's chair. He looked exactly the way Daniel felt: frayed around the edges. George's eyes had acquired a new collection of dark circles and what little hair George had looked lank, dull and even grayer. The man appeared to have aged five years over the course of the day.

Daniel supposed that he seemed even more shell-shocked than George. His confrontation with Lori Dorsett had probably aged him ten years.

She doesn't get it. She thinks she's a warrior for truth. He would have to talk with her again, at the very least put her on his prayer list.

"Okay, guys. Let's begin," Christine said.

Daniel heard excitement in her voice. She wasn't exactly cheerful, but she certainly was enjoying the opportunity to be lawyerly.

Christine laid her hands on top of the papers, as if she were trying to heal them. "I've looked at these documents ten ways to Sunday and I've concluded that we have three options open to us."

"Three is a hopeful number in Christianity," Daniel said. "Many people believe that three is a symbol of the will and purpose of God—from three angels visiting Sarah to three persons in the Trinity."

"Amen," George said softly.

"In this case, numerology leads you astray. Our three options are all rotten."

George groaned.

Christine continued. "We can ask McKinley Investments to reconsider settling with us on the theory that it will make them look good. That's option one.

"Option two is to attack their defense head-on. We can attempt to prove at arbitration that they've guessed wrong about George…in other words, that George was less expert than the article would suggest.

"Option three is not to fight. We crawl away and lick our wounds."

Daniel felt a smile tug at his lips. "I like option one. We appeal to McKinley's better side."

Christine snorted. "Investment firms don't have a better side. They'll probably laugh in our collective faces. Even if they are willing to talk about it, we'll be forced to accept less than sixty percent. Much less."

"Oh." Daniel's momentary restored hope melted like ice cream on a sunny sidewalk.

"The second option is our only choice," George said. "I'll gladly help you prove I don't know what I'm talking about. It won't be hard to do."

"Unhappily, George," Christine said, "discrediting you may be almost impossible. The article speaks for itself." She smiled at George. "I found it online. It's quite informative. We'd have an uphill battle to convince the arbitrator you didn't understand the perils of junk bonds."

Daniel looked at George and saw him staring glumly at a spot on the floor. "Well then, that leaves the third option. We admit defeat and replace the money ourselves." George abruptly stood. "As the church's financial secretary, it will be up to me to raise as much cash as I can. I'll begin a new fund-raising campaign and I'll also write the first check. I have a retirement account I can tap. I'll start with that."

Daniel levered himself out of his chair and put his arm around George's shoulder. "The church is not going to let you give away your retirement money, George. Margo and you are counting on it."

"We've talked about it. She understands what I have to do. After all, I'm to blame for what happened."

Daniel took a step backward. "I won't deny that you're *partially* at fault, George. But Quentin Fisher played a major role in creating the problem, and I deserve a hefty share of the blame. As the church's pastor, I had a responsibility to be more involved. The Elders would be within their rights to send me packing."

"And the congregation would be within its rights to fire the Elders—who *also* should have been watching over our nest egg." Christine leaned back in the swivel chair. Daniel noted that she had stacked the papers on his desktop into four neat piles. "We need to find a solution that gets our money back, rather than worry about who's to blame for the mess."

"Christine is right," another female voice behind Daniel announced. He spun around. Lori stood in the doorway, a determined look on her face. Her eyes seemed puffy. He wondered if she'd been crying and then hoped that she had. To feel nothing after what she'd done would be a terrible commentary on the state of her soul.

She went on. "You need a workable solution that will return your investment. Specifically, you need affirmative proof that Quentin Fisher provided bad information to the church."

Christine spoke first. "If you've come to retrieve the two electronic bugs, Ms. Dorsett, forget it. I have them safely locked up."

Lori ignored Christine and spoke to Daniel. "I didn't want to leave without saying a proper goodbye."

"How did you know where to find me?" he asked.

Lori stepped into the office. "It didn't take much detective work to figure out you would have another meeting to sort things out."

Christine tried again. "You have mind-boggling gall to show your face here. Especially after the damage you've done."

"I'm sorry that I deceived you. But you still may be able to arrange a settlement."

"How?"

"Let me tell you something that you don't know. Quentin filed a report before he died stating that George overruled his investment recommendations. Quentin claimed that he advised the church *not* to buy speculative bonds.

George jumped into the conversation. "That's a lie! He urged me to buy those bonds."

"I believe you," Lori said. "Somewhere there has to be evidence to Fisher's lies. I suggest you find it."

"You're an unusual piece of work, Ms. Dorsett. You agree that Quentin cheated us…that he took advantage of George. Yet you helped gather evidence that blows our case out of the water.

"I did my job—but I don't think what I did made much difference. Even if I hadn't overheard George talk about his article, chances are the same facts would have come out under deposition and cross-examination. Our lawyers would have probed and prodded George Ingles for hours." She smiled. "None of you are very good liars."

Christine rose from her chair and moved around the desk. Her face looked hard. Her eyes flashed darkly. "There wouldn't have been any questions to answer if we had settled the case—as everyone wanted to do before you did your dirty work."

Lori shrugged. "I think our lawyers would have found out about George, anyway."

"Maybe. But on their own, they might not have realized the significance of his article. You heard George describe it. You heard us talk about the implications. You handed it to them on a platter."

"We can debate the fine points of evidence all day and not change each other's minds. I've accomplished what I wanted to do—I've told you that I'm sorry for all that happened. In a few hours, I'll be on a plane to Chicago. Out of Glory and out of your lives, for good."

Daniel noticed that Lori had begun to stare at him. He thought about extending his hand, but couldn't bring himself to do it.

Lori made a soft sigh. "Goodbye, Daniel. I enjoyed the time we spent together."

He finally found his tongue. "You don't have to run away, Lori. I had no right to speak to you like I did earlier."

She shook her head. "Chicago is my home. My friends are there, my life is there." She smiled. "Besides, I'm smart enough to know what small towns are like. Once the word gets around—and it will—the folks in Glory will see me as the evil insurance investigator who harmed the church." She fluttered her fingers at Daniel. "Well, I'd better go while the going's good."

Without another word she turned and left. Daniel watched his office door close behind her and heard her footsteps fade.

He realized that no one had spoken. He looked at Christine and George. They, too, stared into the space Lori had occupied.

In the ensuing silence he could hear the engine in Lori's car start and the car move past his window. Then it was quiet again.

Christine crossed her arms across her chest. "My head wants to say good riddance to bad news," she said, "but my heart actually feels...*sorry* to see her go. I enjoyed her company the other evening. We could have become good friends, maybe, if she hadn't been a spy."

"Christine, you're a big-hearted woman who knows that we've been commanded to forgive our enemies. You're halfway down the road to forgiving Lori." Daniel hesitated. "I'm still sitting in my driveway, feeling furious that she betrayed us. I have a lot of praying to do on the subject."

"I wonder," George said, calmly. "If we'd kept the information to ourselves—well, wouldn't that have been a kind of lie?"

Daniel peered at George for a few seconds, then tossed back his head and laughed. "Well done, George! You're also thinking like a Christian should."

"Pardon me while I throw up." Christine mockingly gagged. "How can I be an effective lawyer if we're all going to be a bunch of Spirit-filled do-gooders?"

Daniel wrapped his arms around Christine and George. "We're going to be okay, my friends." For the first time in weeks, Daniel really believed it.

Why did Glory need a traffic light at the corner of King and Main? Lori wondered as she came to full stop. She decided not to make a turn on red, but to wait for the light to switch to green.

The way people feel about me in this town, I'm likely to get a ticket.

Lori realized that she was no longer welcome in Glory. Christine's harsh words and nasty tone of voice proclaimed that fact loud and clear. So did Daniel's lukewarm farewell—he didn't even offer to shake her hand.

Even worse had been Ann Trask's aggressive rudeness when Lori had walked passed Ann's office on her way out of the building.

"I presume that you're going back to where you came from?" Ann said.

Lori stopped. Ann's expression might have been chiseled in stone. Her eyes looked cold and unfriendly.

"I'm flying to Chicago this afternoon," Lori said.

"Wonderful. We don't need outside troublemakers in Glory."

Lori didn't feel in a mood to argue. "Goodbye to you, too, Ann."

"I wish you'd never come here." Ann's words stabbed like a knife.

"I feel the same way."

"Except, you can fly away free as a bird—we have to clean up the mess you created."

Lori willed herself to control the anger she felt.

"I'm sure that you will manage."

"Oh, we'll manage. People like you have been trying to take down the Church of Christ for two thousand years. Fortunately, you will never succeed."

Lori began to walk forward. How could she explain to Ann what actually happened? How could she try to justify her job?

Ann kept talking. "You know what really bothers me, Miss Dorsett—you've hurt a lovely man."

Lori stopped and faced Ann. "I know, but that wasn't my intention."

"You encouraged Daniel to fall for you as part of your job. I'm sure you can guess what we call that kind of woman in Glory."

Lori didn't respond, for fear that she would end up flattening Ann Trask with a karate chop.

Lori jogged down the hallway, eager to get out of the church.

It comes with the territory. People don't like you to discover their dirty little secrets.

Lori glanced at herself in the car's rearview mirror. Of course Ann's words hurt. But, in time, she'd manage to forget the ache in her heart. She always did. Getting back to her apartment overlooking Lake Michigan had amazing restorative powers. So did thinking about a vacation—or maybe a new sports car.

Except, this time is different.

This time, the "bad guys" were mostly "good guys." And this time, Daniel Hartman was at the center of the situation.

This time, the ache in your heart won't be so easy to soothe.

The light at King and Main turned green. Lori hit the accelerator and turned right. She had almost reached the town limits when an insistent beeping sound caught her ear. She realized that her satellite telephone was ringing.

The only person who had the phone's number was Kevin Pomeroy and she didn't feel in the mood to talk to him right now. The beeping stopped.

Good. I'll call him when I get to the airport.

Lori increased speed on State Route 34A. Glory, North Carolina, would soon be a memory.

The satellite phone began to beep again.

Lori decided that the sat phone was too big to hold while she was driving. She steered the car to the road's shoulder and dug the hefty telephone out of her handbag.

"Yes, Kevin."

"Your flight back to Chicago this afternoon showed up on the department's electronic calendar."

"Fancy that."

"I don't want you to leave Glory yet."

"What?" She heard the pitch of her voice raise an octave. "I'm on my way to the airport as we speak."

"Turn around. The situation has changed."

"How?"

"The information you discovered about George Ingles has been rendered moot."

"What are you talking about, Kevin?"

"I just got word that the auditors finished a detailed review of the investment accounts that Quentin Fisher managed. They found a total of one hundred dollars in the Glory Community Church account. They assume that's the money that George Ingles sent to McKinley Investments to open the church's trust account several months ago. Since then, no other money has been deposited or withdrawn."

"The church bought nearly a million dollars of junk bonds," Lori said.

"Maybe so, but they didn't send any of the purchase money to McKinley Investments."

"That makes no sense, Kevin. The church has a ton of paperwork that confirms the transaction. I saw it barely ten minutes ago."

"And I saw the results of our audit. The church's cash never reached McKinley Investments. And there's no record that McKinley ever purchased the junk bonds in question."

"Something is rotten in Elizabeth City."

"Yep. We may be looking at a wholly different kind of fraud. George Ingles and Quentin Fisher may have been in collusion to cheat McKinley Investments."

"What do you want me to do, Kevin?"

"Stay put for a few days. We may want you to take another, more detailed look at George Ingles."

"That could be difficult—my cover is blown. Big time!"

"Are you sure?"

"Everyone involved knows who I am. You can help remove the tar and feathers when I get back to Chicago."

He paused briefly, growling. "That's the sound I make when I'm grumbling. Coming back home will cost you. Forget the time off. I expect to see you sitting in your office on Monday morning."

"As you wish, my liege." She turned off the phone.

Lori shut her eyes and rested her head on the steering wheel.

Why would the money not pass through the church's account at McKinley Investments? The cash should have been deposited and then used to buy the junk bonds.

A stunningly simple answer blossomed in her mind, and George Ingles had nothing to do with it. She checked her watch. If she was quick about it, she'd have time to tell the folks at the church and still catch her five o'clock flight. She waited until the road was clear and made a sharp U-turn.

Lori could hear Daniel's voice the moment she entered the hallway that led to church's office wing. *Good, they're still here.*

She stepped into Daniel's office without bothering to knock. Three pairs of eyes looked at her in astonishment.

"Lori?" Daniel said as he stood.

Christine, still sitting behind Daniel's desk, jumped in. "Did you forget something, Ms. Dorsett?"

George merely peered at her quizzically.

Lori moved closer to the desk. "There's been an extraordinary piece of late-breaking news. May I look at the paperwork you received from McKinley Investments?"

Christine perused the top of Daniel's desk, stopping to study each of the four stacks to recall, Lori guessed, the papers it contained.

"The first pile contains several items of routine correspondence between Fisher and George Ingles," Christine finally said. "The second is a set of four account statements the church received from McKinley Investments. The third and fourth are instruction sheets that explain how to deposit and withdraw money, and several pieces of legal boilerplate. There's nothing here that McKinley Investments hasn't seen before," she said. "In fact, they generated most of it."

"I want to see your account statements."

Christine pushed the second stack toward Lori. "Knock yourself out."

Lori removed the metal clamp that held the papers together and riffled through the sheets. She noted that Daniel had moved behind her and was watching over her shoulder.

"Can I ask what you're looking for?" Christine said.

"I'm not quite certain," Lori answered as she examined the statements, "but I'll know it when I see it."

"This extraordinary piece of late-breaking news of yours," Christine asked, "when do we get to hear it?"

"In a minute." She held one of the statements up to the

afternoon light streaming through Daniel's window. "Bingo!"

"What did you find?" Daniel asked.

"I'm pretty sure that three of the four statements are fakes." Lori turned to Daniel. "Do you have a magnifying glass?"

"An old one. It's somewhere in my credenza, I think." She smiled at him.

"Ah," he said, "you want me to get it for you."

Lori held another statement up to the light while Christine moved her swivel chair out of the way so that Daniel could rummage through the bottom drawers of the credenza behind his desk. Lori could see a growing expression of excitement on the attorney's face. She had clearly understood Lori's cryptic comment about fake account statements.

Lori smiled again when Daniel handed her an old magnifying glass with an aluminum rim and a black plastic handle. It seemed old and much abused but the lens was free of distortion or chips.

She studied the earliest account statement that the bank had received. It was dated January 30. The printing looked crisp and clean against the smooth gray paper, even under the magnifying glass. She set the statement down on Daniel's desk.

The three other statements—February 28, March 31, April 30—seemed lackluster by comparison. They had been printed on different paper—less smoother surfaced and a darker gray color. Under the glass, the printing looked muddy, less well defined. She placed these statements in a new pile alongside the first.

"Are they fraudulent?" George asked. He had also caught on to the possibilities.

"Without a doubt," Lori answered.

"I take it that our money didn't reach McKinley Investments?" Christine asked.

"The financial audit ordered by the lawyers found that the first one hundred dollars George sent to the firm did. Nothing after that."

"And no subsequent financial transactions or bond purchases?"

"Not a one."

"Hot dog!" Christine shouted.

Daniel moved closer to his desk. "Will one of you financial geniuses please tell me what's going on?"

"Oh, let me—*please*," George said. His eyes glowed with happiness.

"Press on," Lori said.

"Fisher cashed the checks I gave him and kept the money himself," George said to Daniel. "He never deposited the checks in our trust account. Consequently…"

"He didn't buy any junk bonds," Daniel interrupted.

"Not for us, he didn't." Christine said.

"Are we off the hook?" Daniel asked. "Do we get our money back?"

"Well, we're off one hook," Christine said, "but on another." She glanced unhappily at Lori. "Do you want to explain?"

"The audited records don't show what happened to the money, Daniel."

"Stop!" Daniel said. "You guys are moving too fast for me. If there was never any money in our McKinley account, why didn't the firm know that months ago?"

"Because investment firms don't audit client accounts every month," Christine answered. "Quentin Fisher knew that no one would discover the discrepancy until the end of the year."

"I think I understand. The lawyers commissioned a special audit. To prepare for the lawsuit."

"Yep. And now we know that Quentin Fisher misappropriated our money."

"So we'll get it back," Daniel said. "Right?"

"Not necessarily. McKinley Investments may claim that Quentin Fisher and George were in cahoots to steal the money."

"Which we were not!" George interjected.

Lori went on, "I believe you, George, but for the church to recover its money, we'll have to prove that Quentin Fisher pocketed the cash without your knowledge or cooperation."

To her surprise, Lori realized that she'd said "we" instead of "you." Christine, too, must have detected her abrupt shift in loyalties: she grinned at her.

"Does this mean that you'll want to check back into your room at The Scottish Captain?"

Lori thought about it. It would take at least a day, maybe two to help Daniel, Christine and George think through the church's relationship with Quentin Fisher to find the kind of evidence they'd need to prove his criminal intent.

"I suppose I will." She made a mental note to call the airline and reschedule her flight.

"Fine with me," Christine said, "but this time you carry your own bags upstairs."

"It's a deal!" Lori noticed that Daniel was also smiling. *No man who smiles that way is still infuriated at you.* She felt a shiver of delight at the thought.

TEN

Daniel began Monday morning with a visit to Tony Taylor. Perhaps it was the heavy hazy air that day, or perhaps it was Daniel's growing reluctance to spend more time inside the grim facility—for whatever reason, he perceived a smell made of equal parts of decay and despair that seemed to envelop him when he took his seat at the wooden table in the visitors' room.

"Good morning, Tony. You're looking well." Daniel forced himself to smile.

"And you're a rotten liar. But what does it matter how bad I look. You're the only person from the church, other than my wife, who's come to see me recently," Tony said, despondent. "I was beginning to think that Glory forgot all about me."

Daniel stared at his hands resting on the metal table. He should have reminded the congregation what Jesus said about visiting people in prison. It was another important responsibility he'd let fall by the wayside.

Tony half smiled. "At least I have you on my side."

Daniel suffered a second rush of embarrassment— along with a spurt of regret that he had committed himself to the seemingly impossible task of helping Tony clear his name. He felt stymied about what to do next. His meager efforts to date had produced no fruit.

Well, maybe one small piece of fruit. The package of background information provided by Rex Grainger proved an excellent summary of the murder and the cast of characters involved. But he found nothing in the slim stack of paper that might set Tony Taylor free.

Daniel hoped that he didn't look as gloomy as he felt. It was hardly a surprise that he should prove an inept investigator. The Chaplain Corps' training programs didn't teach detecting. If only his stint in the U.S. Army had given him the kind of skills that Lori Dorsett had mastered. She might have found enough proof to get Tony out of jail by now—assuming there was any proof to find.

"I'm a little unsure what my next step will be," Daniel said hesitantly.

Tony nodded glumly and gave another shrug. "Well, at least you're trying. And that gives me some hope."

"There's always hope," Daniel said.

Tony sat up in his chair. "Tell me, what's going on outside these walls that I should know about?"

Daniel leaned across the table and spoke in a softer voice. "We've had a bit of good news at the church. We now know that Quentin Fisher hoodwinked George Ingles right from the get-go. Fisher never deposited our money in the McKinley Investment Trust account. He never bought junk bonds. All but a hundred dollars of our money has disappeared."

Tony's eyes lit up. "Are you telling me that the money was never invested—that we might be able to get it back?"

"The truth is that we don't know what happened to it. I suppose it could be anywhere—from a private bank account in the Caribbean to stuffed inside Quentin Fisher's mattress."

"I hope you guys are looking for it."

"The thought has crossed our mind." Daniel smiled. "It's nice to know that we weren't as stupid as we thought—we were up against a sophisticated thief. We're feeling…optimistic."

He watched Tony's expression darken. "You may feel good about the news," Tony said, "but it puts me into an even deeper hole. If Quentin Fisher had the money all along—maybe buried in his backyard—well, that could give me an even better motive to kill him."

Daniel didn't know how to respond. Tony was right. Once the news of Fisher's larceny got out, the police would think that Tony had an even stronger motive to commit murder.

The darkness in Tony's face seemed to lighten a shade. "Forget what I said—I'm grateful you told me. Now I know where I stand. And I feel pleased for the church. It's nice to know that we stand a chance of getting our money back, even though I may not be around to see it put to work." He managed a weak smile. "I really mean that."

Daniel didn't try to hide the tears that welled in his eyes. "You didn't kill Quentin Fisher, Tony. We're going to find out who did—and get you out of here."

Easier said than done.

Daniel's telephone rang while he was staring out the window, trying to think of a new approach for helping Tony Taylor. He picked up the receiver without checking the Caller ID.

"Good morning, this is Daniel Hartman."

"Hi. It's Lori."

The words made his heart race.

"How are you this lovely morning?" he said.

"Concerned. I just told my boss that I intend to spend another day in Glory. He thinks I'm nuts, because he knows that I no longer have a cover—so I can't keep working as he wanted me to."

Daniel paused to figure out what she'd just said.

"What else did your boss want you to do in Glory?"

"He'd like to find out if George was working with Fisher."

"I can assure you that George could never do anything to harm Glory Community."

Her voice became somber. "The unlikely can become probable when large sums of money are at stake, Daniel. We have to seriously consider all of the possibilities. If George colluded with Fisher to steal the money, the church may not have a claim against McKinley Investments. But if Fisher acted alone, Christine should be able to make a strong argument that McKinley is responsible for the actions of its employee."

"Possibility Number One would certainly make your boss happier," Daniel said, then wished he could take back his words. But he realized that damage had been done when he heard Lori take a deep breath.

"I want you to understand something about my company and my boss—his name is Kevin Pomeroy, by the way. They truly like to pay legitimate claims to honest clients, because that's what an insurance company is designed to do. But they're equally determined not to pay fraudulent claims to thieves."

"I agree," he said feebly.

"Good! Then you'll understand that a serious issue still

lurks in the background. Quentin Fisher was murdered—
which introduces a flood of confusion to the case."

Daniel groaned without meaning to. Lori had no idea
how right she was. No one was more confused than
Reverend Doctor Daniel Hartman.

She continued, "That's why it becomes absolutely essential that we find some solid evidence of Fisher's
crimes. With luck, it will establish the validity of your
claim and exonerate George."

"Poor George," he said with a shake of his head. "I
don't think he'll enjoy his time in the hot seat."

"For what my opinion is worth, I doubt that George
had a scheme going with Fisher. Frankly, I don't see
George as bright enough to be a master criminal."

Daniel laughed. "God help me, but I feel the same way."

"Then we should be able to prove that Fisher acted
alone." She paused. "I hate talking about stuff like this
on the telephone. Can we meet somewhere and talk
face to face?"

"Come to the church."

"I was hoping for more neutral territory. I'm not quite
ready to face Ann Trask again. The last time we met, well..."

Daniel winced as he imagined the confrontation
between Ann and Lori. "Ann can be quite protective of
me," he said.

"*Protective* is the right word."

"Where are you now?"

"I'm parked on Oliver Street, next to Snacks of Glory.
I called with the intent to lure you outside for a stroll. Are
you in the mood for an early lunch?"

"Actually, that sounds like a plan."

"I'll grab a table inside. When can I expect you?"

"I'll leave as soon as I tell Ann that she may have to rescue me if I don't return promptly after lunch."

Daniel waited several seconds for an answer, then finally said. "Are you still there?"

"Barely, but I'm thinking of hanging up on you for that last remark."

"Ah." He couldn't help laughing as he put down the receiver.

Daniel felt glad to have a short walk on his own. He relished the thought of another lunch with Lori Dorsett. But equally important was some time by himself to think. A chance to mull over his jumbled feelings.

You have a tough issue to deal with and no one to talk to about it.

Daniel regretted his own lack of foresight. He'd let himself become so busy during his few years at Glory Community Church that he'd not had the time to make close friends in town. There was no one he knew well enough to share his personal feelings or seek a helping hand in interpreting Scripture.

You're a pastor who needs a pastor.

When he reached the intersection of Oliver and Broad streets, a pickup truck drove past towing a small sailboat. Daniel immediately recalled the five hours he and Lori had spent on *Anticipation*. He'd fallen in love with her that afternoon, but he hadn't told her then.

Today offered another chance to tell her, but he couldn't while two barriers stood in their way. The first, that Lori didn't seem to grasp the genuine problem posed by her job. Lying for a living was hardly a suitable job for a pastor's wife. The second issue, far more significant, was that Lori didn't share his strong faith in the Lord. How could he share his life with someone who kept God at a distance?

Daniel heaved a sigh. He had two good reasons for ending their relationship and one good reason for keeping it: he loved Lori Dorsett more with every passing hour.

I love her, but not what she does or what she believes.

Daniel looked across Oliver Street to the southwest corner of Founders Park. Two women sat on blankets beneath the westernmost tree, watching four young children run after a small dog that seemed to enjoy being chased. Daniel recognized one of the women as a member of his congregation. He waved as he passed by. She waved back.

Daniel stopped outside Snacks of Glory. There was nothing to be done; the decision was already made. Lori and he would work together for a few days and then she would return to Chicago.

"In the long run, that's best for both of us," he murmured.

He pushed open the restaurant's front door.

If it's best, then why do I feel so rotten?

Daniel found Lori at a quiet table in a rear corner. She wore blue jeans and an off-white blouse. The reddish tint she'd acquired during her day on the water had faded to an attractive tan, making her look even more vibrant and healthy. And entirely lovable.

After they ordered Glorious SOGgy Burgers, she spoke first. "I have to thank you."

"No need. You gave me a good excuse to get out of my office on a lovely day."

"That's not what I meant. I need to thank you for taking another chance on me."

"Well…"

"No. I'm serious. I know how you feel about my job. I know you've been struggling to forgive me."

Daniel fought to remain unruffled. Lori's directness was astonishing—but even more surprising was her ability to zero in on what had been bothering him.

"I won't say that it hasn't been a struggle," he said, "but I have forgiven you."

"I'm glad. I don't mind telling you that most of my victims don't forgive me. I say that based on considerable experience."

"Considerable exper…" Daniel began, then suddenly understood. "I see what you mean." He added, "How many people have you deceived over the years?"

"Dozens, certainly, but I went undercover to catch bad guys. And I did it well." She went on, "I know that makes you unhappy."

Daniel glanced at her smile—both contrite and knowing. She seemed to appreciate the depth of the internal conflict that he'd been working to resolve.

How do I even begin?

"May I ask you something?" he said. "How does your job make you feel?"

"Until recently, I saw what I did as productive work that sought truth and justice. I'd go to sleep every night with a clear conscience."

"My conscience is clear, but that does not make me innocent. It is the Lord who judges me." Daniel smiled. "That's from First Corinthians. Chapter four, verse four."

Lori lifted her hands. "I can't keep up with you if you start quoting the Bible, but isn't there a verse somewhere that praises the officials who catch thieves?"

"Probably—but not officials who break other laws to do their good deeds."

"Do you remember our discussion on the sailboat about things not always being what they seem? We both agreed that sometimes there can be good things that merely seem bad."

"Like Lori Dorsett planting bugs, for example?"

"I never *liked* to con people, Daniel, but I thought it came with the territory. I'd figured that I'd never learn the truth if my targets knew that I worked for Chicago Financial Insurance." She grimaced. "It amazes me how often honest people will decide to lie when large sums of money are at stake."

Daniel nodded. Lori was right. He recalled how easy it had been for George, Christine and himself to "suppress" George's magazine article.

"However—" Lori looked into Daniel's eyes "—I promise that I'll never lie to you again."

"I'm pleased to hear you say that, but…"

"But what?"

"I know that I sound like a pastor, but I pray that your repentance will expand to include the whole world. It's not a good thing to intentionally deceive anyone."

"That's important to you, isn't it?"

"Very."

Lori nodded. She cast a sideways glance at him. "Don't we sometimes have to fight fire with fire? I never went undercover for fun. Everything I did was for a good cause. At least, that's what I used to believe."

"My mother often said that the road to hell is paved with good intentions."

"I think your mother was a wise lady."

"You do?" Daniel jerked upright in his chair. "You've been speaking in the past tense. I just realized that."

"I've finally realized that I don't want to spend my life deceiving people." She smiled. "It's not much fun when people hate you. I'll try not to deceive anyone else in the whole wide world. Ever again. I promise."

"Really?"

"One more devious assignment and I'm through."

Daniel felt his brow scrunch. "One more assignment? In Chicago?"

She made a face. "No, silly! In Glory! We have to find the evidence the church needs to get its money back. You and I may need to trick George Ingles—and possibly Christine—to get the job done."

"Me? I have to help you deceive George and Christine?"

"Just a little. The only way my boss will believe that George is not involved is if we find independent evidence of his innocence. We have to uncover the truth by ourselves—without George's participation. We can't give him a chance to concoct phony evidence, even though we know he wouldn't. Same for Christine."

"I see." Daniel took several quick breaths. "Well, that doesn't sound like deception."

"And I obviously need your help. There's not much I can do on my own in Glory, not anymore."

Daniel looked through the front window and saw a tall truck move east on Oliver Street. Lori was right. If he didn't help her, whatever that might entail, the church would be in for a long, bumpy ride.

"Of course I'll help you."

"That's wonderful," Lori said happily.

"Uh…"

"Yes?"

"This is rather awkward." Daniel hoped that the grin on his face didn't look too soppy. "I was going to ask you for your help."

Her eyebrows arched. "Help you? How?"

"You're not the only one who's been playing detective. Tony Taylor asked me to—in his words—'find out what really happened' on the day that Quentin Fisher was murdered."

"Why would Tony ask you for that kind of assistance?"

"Because he wants a friend in his corner, someone who cares about him."

Lori nodded slowly. "That makes sense, I guess. Church people help each other."

"Unfortunately, I don't know what I'm doing. I feel like I'm standing on the wrong bank of a wide river—I don't know how get to the other side."

Lori didn't say anything. Daniel continued. "You, on the other hand seem to understand the art of deception…*I mean detecting*."

He sensed a blush painting his face. "I…uh…I'm sorry."

"Don't be!" Lori laughed. "In my world, deception and detecting usually went hand and hand—as you well know." She touched his arm. "Have you told Rafe Neilson about the sleuthing assignment that Tony gave you?"

"I did. Rafe is a good cop and a good friend. A couple of weeks ago he told me some of the details about the case against Tony Taylor. Nothing out of bounds, of course. I spoke to him again after I met with Tony for the first time. Do you think he might help us?"

Daniel peered at Lori. She didn't seem fazed by his use of the word us. "It never hurts to ask. I'll pay him a visit."

Relief gushed through Daniel. *She's going to help me.*

Lori kept talking. "Let's review the terms of our agreement. I'll be pleased to help you cross your river, and you'll reluctantly help me prove George Ingles innocent. Do we have a deal, Daniel?"

He allowed himself a smile. Why, he wondered, did her dry sense of humor charm him as often as it did?

He began to laugh. Big, deep, belly laughs that would probably bewilder the waiter. He felt even more delighted when Lori began to laugh with him.

Daniel was filled with a new sense of hope. Lori—and God—had resolved the first barrier between them—her job. That left the matter of Lori's faith.

Lord, I'm counting on You to find a way to encourage Lori to invite You back into her life.

ELEVEN

Lori switched on her satellite phone and sat in the wing chair she'd moved alongside the window in her room.

"Hello, Lori," Kevin Pomeroy said. "What's happening?"

"I'm going to spend a few more days in Glory, after all."

"Why bother? You said your cover is blown."

She thought about lying to Kevin, but then decided to tell him the truth.

No more deviousness. No more deception.

"I have an opportunity to dig more deeply into Quentin Fisher's actual relationship with the church, and with George Ingles. Christine Stanton showed me the paperwork the church received from McKinley Investments. Fisher must have falsified the account statements."

"How did you manage that miracle? Based on your earlier calls, I assumed you were persona non grata at the church. Why is the opposition's lawyer willing to cooperate with you?"

"Because she's a smart lady who knows that I'm working to learn the truth about Quentin Fisher. She's betting that the truth will lead to the church's money." Lori had chosen her words carefully. Finding the "truth" about Quentin Fisher didn't imply that she would be looking for evidence to free Tony Taylor.

"Hmm." Kevin seemed about to ask another question. "I guess I can buy that. The whole thing sounds a bit strange, but then so is the world we live in. You have my blessing—spend another day or two in Glory. Keep me informed of whatever progress you make."

Lori hesitated; this was the hard part of the call. "I'll need your help."

"Me? What can I contribute from Chicago?"

"I'll bet you a dollar that McKinley has managed to get hold of the police report on Fisher's murder. I need a copy."

"Why?"

"Because I'm sure that Fisher's death is somehow linked to the money. Everything fits together—I need to find out how."

"Please don't involve yourself in the investigation of Quentin Fisher's murder. An antique boat is an unusual murder weapon and Fisher worked for a well-known company—the explosion was covered by national news media. These reporters are hungry for more information. The last thing we need is your name and picture popping up in newspapers and on TV broadcasts across the country. You'd never be able to work undercover again."

"I have to take that risk if we want to know the truth. It can't be a mere coincidence that Fisher died in an arranged accident a few weeks after he stole a million dollars."

The line fell silent. Lori held her breath.

"Okay," Kevin said, "I'll see what I can do. The fraud control maven at McKinley owes me favor. And I owe you one or two—which you are rapidly using up,"

"Um…Kevin, I need you to make the call immediately." It was a quarter to five in Glory, but thanks to the different time zones, only a quarter to four in Chicago.

He whistled, as he so often did. "Lori Dorsett, you've become a high-overhead employee."

Lori dropped the sat phone into her lap and looked at the open suitcase, open camera case, open computer bag and open purse lying on her bed. She wondered if she should unpack everything again. She pondered the question until, without meaning to, she drifted off into a nap.

Lori awoke in time to hear her satellite telephone make one final ring before lapsing into silence. She glanced at her watch. Seven o'clock. She'd been asleep for nearly two hours and felt both groggy and cotton-mouthed. Instead of immediately returning Kevin's call, she waited to see if he'd left her a message. A moment later the voice mail icon lit up on the phone's front panel.

Lori retrieved the message. "I've done what you asked," Kevin's voice said. "An excerpt of the police report is sitting in your e-mail. I've also had a chance to rethink what you told me earlier. It doesn't make sense to me—unless you left something important out of your explanation. The church folks must know that your primary responsibility is to protect your employer by uncovering *any* facts that Chicago Financial Insurance can use to terminate the church's claim. So, what's in it for them to help you? Why take the risk by joining forces with the enemy?" He chuckled. "I know you like the underdog to win, but you haven't switched sides, have you? I know that we hunters of truth let the chips fall where they may. But my advice to you is, don't let these particular chips fall too far away from the people who pay your salary."

Lori switched off the phone and began to unpack. Why live out of her suitcase? *If* the evidence could be found, it would probably take two, perhaps three days to prove that George had nothing to do with the scam and maybe even figure out what Fisher did with the church's money.

Actually, it's not much of an "if."

Quentin Fisher had been so sloppy when he forged the account statements that he probably left a mountain of other relevant evidence of his crime. Lori began shifting her clothing from the suitcase to the antique chest of drawers, a lovely piece made of maple.

She zipped her empty suitcase closed and hefted it into the small closet. The bigger challenge would be finding friendly evidence about Tony Taylor. Daniel clearly hoped for a miracle, but the police didn't make major mistakes that often. In fact, small-town cops went out of their way *not* to arrest influential locals. The fact they had arrested Tony Taylor suggested that the evidence against him was compelling.

Lori's unplanned nap had proved surprisingly refreshing. She felt wide awake. She logged on to her laptop and downloaded the report that Kevin had sent. As she'd feared, there wasn't much more information than she'd been able to glean from the summary of facts that Daniel had gotten from the local newspaper editor. The police considered the most significant evidence against Taylor to be the garage-door transmitter they'd found hidden in his office. It operated at just the right frequency to trigger the explosion. Taylor had no explanation for it.

The police had investigated Quentin Fisher's background more thoroughly than the newspaper could. The report noted that Fisher had lived on Long Island, near

New York City, for much of his career, that he had owned a powerboat and that he had been a member of the U.S. Coast Guard auxiliary for ten years. The police took this as evidence that Fisher was comfortable around a marina—and as an explanation for his willingness to climb aboard *Marzipan* to wait for Tony Taylor.

A potentially useful fact was that the preliminary arson investigation had been conducted by Howard Winston, Glory's fire chief. His analysis of the explosion and its cause was subsequently validated by a team of arson agents from the North Carolina State Bureau of Investigation.

Two other minor tidbits: Fisher's wife, Andrea, had died a decade earlier. After her death, Fisher had relocated to North Carolina, planning to retire there eventually. Their grown son—Will Fisher, age thirty-three—still lived in the family home on Long Island.

Lori felt in the mood for a cup of coffee. The owner of The Scottish Captain had set up a mini-kitchen for guests on the first floor, in the corner of the rear parlor, that was equipped with a pod machine. She trotted downstairs and brewed a mug of Mocha Java extra-rich.

She thought about returning to her room, but the evening seemed too lovely to spend inside. She chose instead to drink her coffee in the back garden. To her surprise, she found Rafe Neilson alone in the garden, his hands in his pockets, studying a squat dark green shrub. She had met Rafe three days earlier at an afternoon tea that Emma Neilson had served to her guests. Rafe noticed Lori and looked up.

"Do you know what kind of shrub this is?" he asked.

"I haven't a clue. I'm a city girl."

"That's right—you hail from Chicago."

Lori made a snap decision. She had promised to speak to Rafe about Tony Taylor. Why not now?

"Would you have a few minutes, Rafe? I'd like to chat with you."

He smiled at Lori—a brilliant smile that made his face look even more handsome. Rafe was tall and athletic, obviously in great shape. He had sandy-colored hair and big hazel eyes. In short, one good-looking cop.

Lori realized that she hadn't even felt a flutter. Rafe Neilson's good looks hadn't revved her engine.

Oh, boy! You've definitely fallen for Daniel.

"I have plenty of time," Rafe said. "Emma and I plan to go to a late dinner after she finishes an inventory of the pantry." He tilted his head quizzically. "But, won't I be taking a big risk talking to Lori Dorsett? According to the latest unimpeachable gossip, you're a high-powered secret agent, possibly a foreign spy, sent to Glory to infiltrate our churches."

"Word gets around."

"Within milliseconds, in a town this small."

"I'm afraid that the truth is somewhat less exciting than the gossip. I'm an investigator for Chicago Financial Insurance Company—my specialty is insurance fraud."

Rafe peered at Lori. "You have the look of a former cop. What's your history?"

"I was a member of the 701st Military Police Group. I retired as a warrant officer."

"That's the U.S. Army Criminal Investigation Command Headquarters at Fort Belvoir, Virginia." He laughed. "Now I'm really impressed! You're an alum of one of the best police units in the country. No wonder people are so mad at you. You know what you're doing."

"Apparently so do you. Daniel says that you're a smart and sensible cop—as well as his friend."

"I like to think that both are true."

"I believe you've heard that Tony Taylor asked Daniel to play detective in his behalf?"

Rafe made a soft moan. "Daniel mentioned the possibility, but I didn't take him seriously." He threw in a brief groan. "We seem to have an emerging epidemic of amateur detectives in Glory. Last fall my wife to-be dabbled in crime; this spring my pastor caught the bug."

"I'll try to keep Daniel out of trouble. He asked me to tag along—as a kind of consultant."

"And naturally you agreed?"

"Like you, I consider Daniel to be my good friend."

"I see. Well, I won't insult you by pointing out that you don't hold a North Carolina private investigator's license."

"Daniel isn't a client. He's a concerned pastor who needs a helping hand to watch over one of his flock."

"Glory also seems to be chock-full of good Samaritans."

"I promise to stay out of your way."

"That will definitely maintain our good relationship."

"Of course, it would be useful to know the areas of the investigation that you've carved out as your territory."

Rafe laughed again. "You have an clever way of asking what I know. I've never heard an oblique question phrased like that before." He stopped smiling. "I'm curious. Is your primary objective to help Daniel, or are you more interested in minimizing the insurance liability of that long-named company you work for?"

"Whew! I didn't see that coming." She took a breath. "Now that I think about it, you don't look—or talk—like a small-town cop. What's *your* history?"

"New York State Police. I've handled lots of white-collar crime over the years."

"I'll bet you're good at it."

"You'd win." He pursed his lips. "By the way, you didn't answer my question. What are your priorities?"

"The truth is, I'm split. Besides helping Daniel and uncovering fraud, I'd like to see the church get its money back."

"You think the three things are related?"

"Don't you? Ah. You haven't heard the latest. The junk bonds were never purchased. Fisher apparently pocketed the church's money."

Rafe became silent for a few seconds. "Well, well," he finally said, "that could change some of our thinking. At the very least, it raises a few new questions. First, how involved was George Ingles in the scam?"

"We believe George Ingles was duped by Quentin Fisher."

Rafe grunted. "Second, did Tony Taylor know that Fisher took the money, rather than invest it in junk bonds?"

"Probably not. Quentin Fisher made his dealings look like a conventional investment transaction. He even forged phony account statements."

Rafe nodded. "Third, what became of the money?"

"I'd guess it's in an offshore bank account. Or maybe buried in Fisher's backyard." She added, "How thoroughly did you browse through his house in Hertford?"

Rafe, plainly embarrassed by the question, gazed at the unidentified shrub. "We never searched Fisher's house. There didn't seem to be a reason to back then. As far as I know, the house has been sealed since his death."

"Can you get us inside, for a quick browse-around?"

He immediately looked back at Lori. *"Me?* No way! Talk to the executor of Fisher's estate, whoever that is."

"Fair enough. I'll track him or her down."

"Look—North Carolina's breaking-and-entering laws are strictly enforced in this corner of the state. Get permission, or you'll get yourself arrested."

Lori held up her right hand. "I will not enter Quentin Fisher's house without permission. I promise."

"Why don't I believe you?"

"Because you're a skeptical, case-hardened cynic."

"There is that."

Lori murmured too softly for Rafe to hear, "And because it's the only way."

Lori awoke early, dressed quickly and ate a light breakfast on Tuesday morning—even though her meeting with Daniel to tour the Glory at Sea Marina was set for 10:00 a.m.

They had planned the visit before she'd left the church the day before. "If I'm going to help you effectively," Lori had said, "I need to see the crime scene in person."

Daniel had volunteered to make the arrangements with Rebecca Taylor. "I'll meet you outside the marina's front gate at ten," he'd said clearly and distinctly. Why then was she lounging in a chair at eight forty-five, hoping that the hands of her wristwatch would move more quickly?

Because you're eager to see him again. Too eager! Now you have an hour to kill.

Lori contemplated the best way to pass the time. She'd read the police report three times. She didn't have any shopping to do. She wasn't in the mood for another stroll around Glory or an early morning drive.

Do something useful for the investigation.

Lori sat up straight. There was something she wanted to do—someone she needed to see.

Of course! The fire chief.

Lori recalled that the Glory Fire Department was headquartered on Campbell Street, on the west side of town. If Howard Winston would agree to see her on short notice, she'd have more than enough time for a quick chat. She considered calling to make an appointment, but decided that showing up on his doorstep was the wiser strategy. He'd probably listened to the same gossip that Rafe Neilson had heard.

Fifteen minutes later Lori was ushered into the chief's office by a uniformed fireman who looked about fifteen years old. Winston stood and moved from behind his desk to greet her. He was tall and broad, in his mid-fifties, with a craggy face, graying hair and a leathery complexion. He had, Lori thought, the caring, competent look that every fire chief should exhibit. She shook his hand, sat and explained the purpose of her visit.

"I understand that you have questions about the explosion of Tony Taylor's boat," he said, "but I'm still hazy about why I should answer them."

"Because you're a friend of Tony Taylor. And because I'm working with Daniel Hartman to prove Tony's innocence."

"Both of those reasons get my attention, but neither is good enough to make me jeopardize a prosecution. There's lots about the case that I can't discuss with anyone."

"Fair enough. I won't expect you to answer any question that falls into that category."

Winston nodded. "What do you want to know?"

"Let's start with the general problem of explosions aboard small powerboats—how common are they?"

"*Marzipan* represents the second explosion of its kind that I know of at the Glory at Sea Marina. Fortunately they don't happen every day. Any time gasoline spills into a boat's bilge—its basement, so to speak—you can get an explosive mixture of gasoline vapor and air inside the boat. A cup of gasoline, fully vaporized and mixed with air, has the explosive power of a several sticks of dynamite."

"Yikes."

"Yup. Any spark will initiate a blast. It doesn't happen often, because most boat owners understand the risks. And small boats are required to have bilge blowers as part of their safety equipment. They're designed to dissipate any gasoline vapor before the boat is operated."

"Where does spilled gasoline come from?"

"Gasoline lines can leak and owners accidentally overfill gas tanks—in my experience, those are the two common sources."

Lori moved her visitor's chair closer to the chief's desk. "Quentin Fisher was a member of the Coast Guard auxiliary. Wouldn't he know all about the dangers of spilled gasoline?"

"Absolutely! But as I understand it, he didn't trigger the explosion aboard *Marzipan*."

"Is everyone confident that the blast was caused by gasoline in the boat's bilge?"

The chief hesitated. "Not quite." He drummed his fingers on the table a moment. "I guess it won't do any harm telling you that we now have a different theory. As near as we can figure, the gasoline was in the secondary bilge under the floor of the boat's cuddy cabin—that's the small cabin up front. We think those gas vapors fueled the explosion."

"Why does it make a difference?"

"Well, both the gas line and the gas tank are in the back of the boat. You'd expect to find an accidental gasoline spill in the rear bilge, not the small bilge under the cuddy cabin."

"That would prove the spill wasn't accidental."

"I don't think I can add anything more in that direction."

She smiled at him. "I only have two more questions. Where was Quentin Fisher when *Marzipan* exploded?"

The chief exhaled slowly. "We haven't said anything about that publicly, but his location is fairly obvious. He had to be inside the cuddy cabin when the fumes detonated."

"Perhaps I'm thick—but what makes it 'fairly obvious'?"

"The explosion propelled debris in all directions. If Fisher had been in the boat's cockpit or standing on her deck, well…"

"He would have been blown away from the boat."

"Correct. We found his remains inside the hull." He leaned back in his chair. "And your last question is?"

"What does an explosive mixture of gasoline vapor and air smell like?"

"Haven't you ever smelled spilled gasoline at a gas station, or when someone's refilling a lawnmower?"

"I have. It's not very pleasant. In fact, the smell made me nauseated."

"Multiply that odor ten times. There's your answer."

Lori thanked Chief Winston and left, not completely certain what her visit had accomplished. Two things she had learned were downright confusing. Why would a knowledgeable boater like Quentin Fisher go aboard a boat that reeked of gasoline fumes? And why would he stay on board—and even go below, down into the boat's cuddy cabin, where the gasoline vapor would smell much worse?

"We need solid answers to both questions," she murmured.

This case is getting interesting, she thought as she started her car. In fact, it's beginning to look like Tony Taylor didn't murder Quentin Fisher.

TWELVE

Daniel peered through the chain-link fence at the Glory at Sea Marina. The facility seemed surprisingly uninviting this morning, perhaps because he and Lori had come to investigate a murder rather than go boating.

Or maybe it's the fast-rising heat and humidity?

Today was forecast to be first scorcher of the season— high temperatures made more oppressive by a cloudless sky and the absence of any breeze. Even at 10:00 a.m. the air felt hot and sticky.

Daniel had parked his car on Water Street behind Lori's rental. Once again, they had both arrived for their date a few minutes early. Lori carried a medium-size canvas tote. He'd seen her drop her digital camera and a bottle of water inside. He wondered if she'd also brought any of her high-tech detective gadgetry with her.

Of course she didn't. She promised an end to trickery and dishonesty.

Daniel mopped his brow, surprised at how fresh Lori looked. He had come out in dark khaki trousers and a light blue cotton business shirt, while she had been wise enough to wear shorts and an airy blouse. But at least he'd remembered to dab on plenty of sunscreen. Today there would be no red blotches on his face and arms.

He glanced at Lori. She was obviously enjoying her role as consulting detective.

"We're here to walk in Quentin Fisher's footsteps," she said excitedly. "We want to understand what he was thinking on the day he died, and why he did the things he did."

"Where do we begin?"

"In the upper parking lot—wherever that is. That's where Quentin parked his car."

"*Upper* is a relative term," he said. "Water Street is only about ten feet above sea level. The upper parking lot is just inside the front gate."

She walked away, giving Daniel an excellent view of her suntanned legs. He forced himself to look at Albemarle Sound, smooth and as flat as a paved road, with nary a boat in sight.

"Don't just stand there watching the scenery," Lori called. "We have work to do."

"I'll be right there." He caught up with her in the parking lot. She was scanning her surroundings and taking pictures with her fancy digital camera.

"Where in this lot do you suppose Fisher parked?" she asked.

"I have no idea. The notes I got from Rex Grainger weren't specific."

"Neither was the police report."

"You've seen the police report?"

"Don't sound so amazed. I read an abridged copy last night."

"Which you got from…"

"Kevin, my boss, who in turn borrowed it from

McKinley Investments—but you're wasting valuable brainpower on worthless details. The question you should be asking yourself is, why did Quentin Fisher park so far from the docks?"

Daniel thought about it. "Fisher probably took the first available parking spot he saw when he drove through the front gate."

She shook her head. "He was invited for a brief meeting with Tony Taylor, aboard a boat." She gestured toward the marina office. "He had a map of the marina—supposedly faxed to him by Tony—that depicted all of the parking areas. Why not park down there, closer to the piers?"

Daniel shrugged. "Beats me. Maybe he wanted to stroll around the marina?"

"Have you ever parked up here?"

"Sure. This is considered the long-term parking lot. I park here if I know I'll be out on the water for a night or two."

"Long-term lot—how interesting. And suggestive."

"Suggestive of what?"

Lori turned away instead of answering the question. "The next thing Quentin did was to ask directions from a man who works in the machine shop. Where's that?"

"It's the large building with the green roof."

She walked toward the building, pausing occasionally to take more pictures. Daniel followed close behind, striving to keep his mind on murder.

Lori abruptly stopped. "Here's a likely spot where the impromptu meeting took place. We're parallel to the door to the machine shop—but we're still a long way from the docks."

"Is that important?"

"Definitely—considering the strange conversation Fisher had with the machinist."

Daniel felt himself frown. "What's weird about asking for directions?"

She reached into her canvas tote and brought out a small black notebook. She smiled wryly at Daniel. "One simply cannot conduct a *proper* investigation without a classic black notebook."

She opened it to a page full of neat writing. "According to the police report, Fisher said, and I quote, 'I'm here for a meeting with Tony Taylor aboard *Marzipan*. Do you know where I can find E Dock and *Marzipan*?' The employee replied, 'I think Tony Taylor is out testing a repair job. E Dock is the pier on the right—just like on your map. *Marzipan* is in the first slip.'" She glanced sideways at Daniel. "Don't you find that exchange odd?"

"Nope. I seem to be missing something."

"Well, to begin with, why tell a man covered with grease that you have a meeting with the marina's owner?"

"Politeness?"

"I don't think so. Fisher could have merely asked directions to Tony's office, but he didn't. Why would a machinist care about his appointment with Tony?"

Daniel began to understand Lori's reasoning. "Now that you mention it, it does seem a bit strange. That's the kind of statement Fisher would have made at the marina office."

"Exactly. And why ask a guy who works in the machine shop where a specific boat is located? Wouldn't it make more sense to check with the helpers at the gas dock? Those employees would be able to guide you directly to the boat you're looking for."

"Do you think the machinist lied to the police?"

"Nope. I think that Fisher chose his words carefully."

"For what purpose?"

"I'm not sure—yet."

"How does any of this concern Tony Taylor?"

"I'm not sure of that, either."

"Yet?"

"Absolutely." She poked Daniel's arm. "Let's look at the pier where *Marzipan* was docked."

Lori made for E Dock, with Daniel tagging along. His mind had begun to whirl. The "simple facts" he'd learned from Rafe Neilson and Rex Grainger now seemed coated with a veneer of complexity. Lori was right. Why would Quentin Fisher park in the long-term lot—a hundred yard walk to E Dock? And why would he announce his meeting plans to a marina employee?

And—Daniel suddenly had a new thought—why would Fisher ask questions at all when he had a picture map of the marina in his hand?

Daniel felt a burst of optimism. Seeing the world through Lori's eyes put a new perspective on the evidence the police had collected.

Let's see how many more "simple facts" are up for grabs.

When they reached E Dock, Daniel kept several paces away while she examined—and photographed—a large charred area on the deck planking close to the first slip. "The explosion must have dropped a mass of flaming materials on the dock," she said.

"The pier is made of wood. Why didn't the whole marina go up in flames?"

"Because the decking has been treated with a flame-retardant chemical. I'd say the planking has a 'Class 1' rating—as good as it gets for wood." She added, "The real danger was that the fire aboard *Marzipan* would spread to other boats."

"Fortunately, *Marzipan* was docked in relatively shallow water. There weren't any other boats close to her."

"Do you really think 'fortunately' is the right word?"

"What are you getting at?"

"We'll talk about that some other time." She spun around on her heels. "Right now, I want to test out the police theory that Tony blew up the boat and with a garage-door transmitter." She smiled at Daniel. "You be *Marzipan*. Stand at the edge of the dock, but don't fall in."

Daniel took up position. Lori walked backward off E Dock until she was about fifty feet away from Daniel. "This is about the maximum range for the garage-door transmitter," she said. "Do you agree?" She snapped a photograph.

"Looks right to me." Daniel had an idea. "Except—I suppose that Tony could have been under the dock, in the water."

"No way! Tony appeared a couple of minutes after the explosion. He was dry when he climbed out of the boat he was testing." She laughed. "And before you invent an alternative explanation, he didn't have enough time to take off wading boots, jump into a boat and motor around to the front of the marina."

"But if Tony was standing there, wouldn't somebody have seen him?"

Lori moved closer to Daniel. "You'd certainly think so. According to the police report, there were two dock boys on the gas dock that morning and nine owners working aboard their boats. They all came running when *Marzipan* exploded." She made a face. "I'll bet that the police believe someone saw Tony trigger the explosion but hasn't come forward."

"Because he or she wants to protect Tony."

"Correct." She made a vague gesture. "Now here's where the police have to do a lot of hand-waving. The theory is that Tony detonated the device, then ran to another pier where he had another boat waiting, then motored around the five long docks, making it look like he came from outside the marina. All without being seen."

"When you put it that way, it doesn't seem likely at all." Daniel smiled. "Is the state's case against Tony Taylor really as weak as you make it sound?"

"I think so—and it's even more improbable when you take a closer look at what happened aboard *Marzipan*. You're a sailor. Would you climb into a runabout that reeked of gasoline and go below?"

"No way!" He added, "The police have to know that that doesn't make much sense."

"The police seem to have ignored lots of circumstantial details that don't fit their theory of the case."

"You don't sound surprised."

"I'm not, because I've seen it happen before. The police have a piece of compelling evidence and a strong motive—they assume that the other facts will eventually fit together." She glanced at the marina office. "Tony Taylor is in jail chiefly because the cops found the right garage-door transmitter tucked behind his credenza. They also believe that Tony had a powerful motive for killing Quentin Fisher."

Daniel tsked softly, his heart sinking once again. He'd almost forgotten about the transmitter. "That transmitter seems to be an insurmountable bit of evidence."

"Do you think so?"

"Don't you?"

"Well, you can buy a similar transmitter at any home improvement store."

"I can't keep up with you."

"I'm beginning to feel confident that I know what happened to Quentin Fisher. But I don't know why—not yet."

"Did Tony Taylor murder Fisher or not?"

"Almost certainly not."

"What makes you say so?"

"Think it through, Daniel. You know everything that I do."

"You are absolutely infuriating!"

She wrinkled her nose in imitation disapproval. *"Moi?"*

"What do we do next?" he asked.

"I have one final loose end to tie up. I need to see the inside of Tony Taylor's office."

Daniel tried to read Lori's face. She seemed sure of herself, but this was the first demonstration he'd seen of Lori's skills as a detective. She could talk the talk and walk the walk—God willing, the results would match her bravado.

"Have you ever met Rebecca Taylor?" he asked.

"Nope. We glared at each other each other from a distance that day you took me sailing."

"Can I tell her that you're assisting me?"

"Probably not a good idea—you would have too many details to explain. Tell her that you dropped in to say hello. It's the truth."

Daniel nodded and offered his arm. "Onward and upward."

He led Lori up the wooden stairway to the marina's business office. She stepped inside first and placed her camera back in the canvas tote. She seemed to rummage for something inside the bag, but then apparently changed her mind.

The visit was over in three minutes. Daniel introduced Lori, exchanged a bit of small talk with Rebecca and gave her a big hug before they left. Lori stood two paces behind Daniel and smiled for the duration. The only time she spoke was to ask a single question. "Did Quentin Fisher ever visit Tony in his office?"

Daniel bit his tongue. Rebecca stared at Lori, seemingly growing more annoyed as each second ticked past.

"Why would you want to know that?" Rebecca said.

"The answer may help Tony—although I can't tell you how today."

Rebecca shrugged. "I don't believe you, but I can't see that the answer makes any difference. Yes—Fisher visited the marina about a month ago."

"What was that all about?" Daniel asked as they trudged up the slight slope to their cars parked on Water Street.

"I needed to check out the burglar alarm system. All the security seems focused on the main room where the file cabinets, safe and cash register are located. Tony's office has very little protection—there's an ancient magnetic switch on the window, but no motion detector to pick up an intruder in the room.

"Someone who knew what he was doing—and that there's no motion detector—could easily defeat the magnetic switch and get into Tony's office. All he'd need would be a thin-bladed knife and a tall enough ladder—and there are ladders lying around everywhere in a boatyard."

"What's to steal in Tony's office?"

"I didn't say anything about stealing. There are other reasons to break in to a locked office."

"Will you stop being cryptic and say what you mean…" All at once Daniel understood. "It can't be that simple."

"I think it is."

"But why?"

"I have no idea. We'll have to find a way to get Tony out of jail, and once we do, we'll probably also learn what happened to the church's money."

Daniel grunted. "Are you sure it's that easy to break into Tony's office? Could there be—" he reached for the right word "—hidden gadgets to catch burglars."

"I'll know if there are later today."

"Later?"

"As soon as I examine the pictures I took with the miniature digital camera sewn into the handle of my canvas tote. Did you notice that I kept shifting the bag? I photographed Tony's entire office."

"You're incorrigible!"

"I prefer to think of myself as effective."

"You promised me there'd be no more dishonesty."

"Shooting a few candid photos is *hardly* dishonest."

"I was going to offer to buy you lunch, but now I'm not so sure."

"In that case," she said cheerfully, "I'll buy you lunch—as my way of making amends for shocking your sensibilities."

Daniel knew that he had stopped smiling at Lori. "My sensibilities are not the problem, here. It's your way of thinking that needs lots of remedial work."

* * *

Lori pushed open the door to her room at The Scottish Captain, sank into the antique winged-back chair and kicked off her sandals hard enough to make them skitter under the bed.

How can Daniel object to a minor deception that will help get an innocent man out of jail?

Lori lifted her feet atop her bed and snuggled them into her soft comforter. Pure heaven.

He's a pastor. Maybe he can maintain higher standards than the rest of us. But it's not fair to impose them on me. Not when I'm helping him help one of his parishioners.

The air conditioner in the room—a European-style unit that stood in the corner—blew cold air on her face. Lori felt the tension acquired at lunch seep out of her.

She had suggested that they eat at the Glorious Catch, down the street from the marina. Their meals were merely okay—not worth their high price and certainly not worthy of the praise that Christine Stanton heaped on the restaurant.

To make matters worse, they had both been on edge— both trying to steer the discussion to prove their points.

Lori had said, "I know that you don't like the argument that the means justify the ends, but sometimes the greater good requires that a person tells a lie."

"You can find an interesting example of that point of view in the Bible. You can read the story of Rahab in the second chapter of the Book of Joshua as evidence that lies may be necessary in extreme situations."

"What's the story?"

"Read it for yourself. That's the best way for you to reach your own conclusions." Daniel had frowned. "It's actually child's play to invent circumstances that seem to prove that it's okay to deceive other people. All you need is a situation that balances a convenient lie against serious harm. For example, few of us would say it's right to tell a lynch mob where an intended victim is hiding. And you might want to deceive an enemy in wartime to save lives. And I suppose that you shouldn't tell a good friend what you truly think about the new hair color she loves."

"So, it seems that we really don't disagree."

"No, I'm afraid we do. I grant that there are situations where we may be forced to lie—but necessity doesn't make it right. The Bible teaches that lying is never a good thing to do. 'The righteous hate what is false,' that's from Proverbs 13:5."

"Doesn't that strike you as a silly argument?" she had countered. "It can be simultaneously right and wrong to deceive someone."

"I see it as more challenging than silly. Theologians have wrestled with this issue for thousands of years. You and I are not going to come up with a definitive answer."

"I guess we'll have to agree to disagree."

"I guess we will."

There'd been a noticeable chill between them when they'd parted. He had clomped away in his direction, she had stormed off in hers.

Lori kicked angrily at the bedclothes, sending the comforter sliding sideways. "Let him ask Tony Taylor," she said out loud. "See if he minds a bit of deception if it will get him out of jail."

Lori's eyelids felt heavy. She swallowed a yawn and decided to make her daily call to Kevin Pomeroy. She dialed her satellite phone. Kevin answered on the second ring.

She started speak a hello when Kevin brusquely cut her

off. "Are you still in Glory?" he barked. Lori could feel his anger coursing toward her from Chicago.

"Yes, I am," she said evenly.

"Fly back to Chicago tomorrow morning. I expect to see you sitting in your office tomorrow afternoon."

She took a long, deep breath. Kevin rarely got bossy, but when he did, he became insufferable.

"I asked you for time off, remember?"

"Time off is sitting on a beach. Time off is shopping for a new car. Time off is *not* working as in investigator for a church that is suing one of our clients."

"I explained all this the last time we spoke."

"No! You conned me the last time we spoke. You have switched sides."

"It's inconvenient for me to leave Glory today or tomorrow," she said, her voice remaining calm. "I'm very close to resolving the case. That's why I need to ask another favor from you."

"Another favor? You can't be serious."

"It's a simple request, Kevin. I need you to contact McKinley Investments, find out who is the executor of Quentin Fisher's estate and then get me permission to enter Fisher's house in Hertford, North Carolina."

She heard a loud snorting noise and imagined his face becoming bright red. "No more favors, no more time off, no more letting you support that church at the expense of our company." He paused, then said, "I want you back in Chicago. That's not a suggestion, it's an order."

"I'm sorry, Kevin," she said. "I can't come back yet. A man's future is at stake, along with the church's financial health. You have to trust me on this. I'm not hurting the company by helping the church."

He muttered something she didn't catch. The line went dead before she could ask Kevin to repeat himself.

Congratulations, Lori Dorsett. It looks like you're about to start a new job. I wonder what it will be.

Lori spent the rest of afternoon in her room, mostly reading magazines. When suppertime rolled around, she ate the last of her granola bars, drank bottled water and watched a DVD of *Sleepless in Seattle* on her laptop computer. It was one of three Meg Ryan movies she'd packed—just in case. Lori considered topping a double-feature with *You've Got Mail* or *When Harry Met Sally* but found her mind repeatedly drawn back to the name Daniel had mentioned. *Rahab.* The more she tried to ignore the woman, the louder "Rahab" seemed to echo across her consciousness.

Who is Rahab? And why does she rate space in the Bible?

Lori knew there was a Bible in the same drawer as the local telephone book. Reluctantly she retrieved it and tried to remember what Daniel had told her. She riffled though the more than one thousand pages. The story of Rahab could be anywhere.

She dialed Daniel's cell phone. Five rings, then a voice thick with sleep said, "Daniel Hartman."

Oh, no! I woke him up.

"I'm sorry I disturbed you, Daniel. This can wait until morning."

"I don't usually go to bed this early. I dozed off in a chair." He coughed softly. She heard him clear his throat. "Okay I'm awake now."

"This may sound silly," Lori said, "but I want to read about the Rahab woman you mentioned earlier. I don't know where to find her in the Bible."

"That's not silly at all." His voice now seemed full of enthusiasm. "Joshua is the sixth book of the Bible, in the Old Testament. Most of Rahab's story is in Chapter Two. You'll enjoy it. The first half of Joshua reads like a modern adventure novel—complete with spies who infiltrate enemy territory and spread disinformation to prevent attack."

"Right up my alley."

"Now that you mention it…" His tone had become thoughtful. "Call me after you read the chapter. Tell me what you think."

Once Lori began reading, she remembered the story from Sunday School. Rahab—a prostitute in Jericho—hid Joshua's spies on her roof and sent the king's soldiers on a wild-goose chase when they came to arrest the Israelites. She did this to gain favor with Joshua, who later spared her life and everyone else in her house when the city walls came tumbling down.

She closed the Bible. Rahab's story certainly seemed to prove the value of a good lie at the right time—and yet something about Rahab's tale was different than her own. Lori spent ten minutes figuring out what it was.

She called Daniel.

"I think I get it, now. Rahab practiced deception, but she didn't glorify what she did or claim it was morally right. I, on the other hand, tend to be delighted when I successfully deceive people. And why not? I've usually received raises and bonuses as rewards for lying creatively."

"Yeah, that's it!" he said. Lori heard him yawn. "Sometimes it's necessary to lie—but don't fall into the trap of thinking that lying is a good thing or that you haven't sinned by doing it." He added, "Congratulations, you've just completed your first Bible study in…"

"Twenty-four years."

"And you received an A." He yawned again. "Well, let's talk tomorrow. I'm heading for bed."

"Not until we talk about our trip to Hertford tomorrow."

"Hertford? Why are we going to Hertford?"

"Joshua sent two spies to 'Go, look over the land.' You and I are going to go and look over Quentin Fisher's house."

Lori heard a clunk over the telephone. "Give me a moment," Daniel said, "I knocked an empty cup off my nightstand. Where were we? Oh, yes, you were telling me that you have permission to view Quentin's house."

"Actually, I don't have permission, but that's no problem because I'm part of the investigative team that's sort of on Quentin Fisher's side, if you know what I mean."

"Oh, I know exactly what you mean. However, I should explain that I got a telephone call from Rafe Neilson today. He specifically said that I should not take part in any—and I quote, 'harebrained attempts to break and enter Quentin Fisher's home.' He explained that the local cops will happily arrest pastors and pests."

Lori shook her head. "He actually said 'pests'?"

"Indeed he did. He also warned me that you have breaking and entering on your mind."

"A gross untruth. I specifically said that we will look over Quentin's house. I never said that we'd go inside, although I admit I'd like nothing better."

The line fell silent, but she could still hear him breathing. "I'll probably regret asking, but just how is it possible to look over the house without going inside?"

"You'll see tomorrow. For now, let's just say that I have a couple of other interesting gadgets in my camera case that will come in handy."

"No breaking and entering?"

"I wouldn't dream of it."

"And our *non*-breaking and *non*-entering will somehow help the church?"

"And perhaps even Tony Taylor."

"How?"

"I'm not quite sure—but call it a hunch if you'd like, or even woman's intuition. I'm certain that we have to look around that house."

"I hope you know what you're doing."

"Excuse me, Colonel Hartman," she said with mocking officiousness. "You of all people should know that I've received excellent training in investigative procedures."

"Hmm. When will we conduct this...uh, mission, Special Agent Dorsett?"

"Tomorrow, Sir, at your convenience. When are you available to reconnoiter?"

"Not until thirteen hundred hours."

"I'll pick you up in front of the church promptly at 1:00 p.m., Sir."

"Roger that. Good night, Lori,"

"Good night, Daniel. *Hoo-rah!*"

Daniel laughed. Lori hung up the telephone and wondered how Rahab would have described tomorrow's "mission."

She abruptly realized that she knew who to ask.

"Lord," she said softly. "I have a question about Rahab. But first we have to chat about a few other things."

THIRTEEN

Daniel watched the blue rental car move north on King Street. He sensed his heart beating quickly. He felt nervous, excited, more than little jazzed.

All the emotions of a real combat mission. Daniel knew better, of course. A slightly unofficial visit to a house in Hertford, only twenty miles to the northwest of Glory, carried none of the risks of Operation Desert Storm—but why not enjoy the thrill that seemed to knot itself around his stomach?

Simply thinking about Lori Dorsett caused him to smile. And he'd been smiling more than usual lately.

Daniel had been standing out of sight in the rear entrance to Glory Community Church. He moved forward and waved as Lori drove into the parking lot.

"You look like the proverbial cat who's caught the canary," she said as he climbed into the passenger's seat. Daniel noted that she wore blue jeans, a green shirt and huge mirrored sunglasses.

"I'm happy because we're doing something proactive to help Tony Taylor and the church," he said. "However, I'm also unhappy because I don't have a pair of those funky Smokey the Bear shades."

"Says who?" Lori used her right hand to point to the floor in the back of the car. "Reach into my canvas tote bag."

Daniel followed her instructions and found a red plastic eyeglass case sitting on top of a laptop computer. He undid the plastic catch.

"You bought me new sunglasses?" He couldn't keep the amazement out of his voice.

"They're necessary equipment this afternoon. We'll be viewing a laptop computer screen outdoors on a bright day. These mirrored lenses do a good job of eliminating glare."

"If I asked what we'll see, I don't suppose you'd tell me."

"Why bother? We'll be in Hertford in twenty minutes and then all will be clear."

Daniel pushed forward against his seat belt so that he could see the road behind in the side mirror.

"Relax, Daniel. No one is following us. We're simply a couple of ordinary folks out for a pleasant afternoon drive in the country."

He muttered, "Oh, how I wish that were true."

"Did you say something?"

"Not I." He leaned his head back against the headrest and cast a glance at Lori. Her expression, once playful, had now become resolute. He guessed that she also felt on edge. She would probably stay that way until their "mission" was over. He offered up a silent prayer. *God, be with us this afternoon. I don't really know what Lori's plan is, but I ask Your blessing on our undertaking. May our work today be pleasing to You. And—please keep us safe and out of jail. Amen.*

Daniel tried to recall the number of times he'd been to Hertford. Three, possibly four. The town was smaller than Glory—a population of only two thousand—yet it was the home of county government. If Tony Taylor was tried for murder, it would be in the Perquimans County Courthouse in Hertford.

"I hope Quentin Fisher didn't live in downtown Hertford," he said. "We don't need an audience of neighbors watching as we peruse his property."

"As a matter of fact, he lived on a road that leads deep into the Great Dismal Swamp. I'm guessing the houses each sit on several acres of land." She tapped his arm. "Reach down into my bag again and find a folded sheet of paper. I downloaded a map of the area and printed it out. Quentin's house is marked with a red X."

Daniel retrieved the map. "Now that's interesting—we're looking for Kelly Lane, which is off Don Juan Road." He chuckled. "I wonder how Don Juan ended up in North Carolina?"

"I assume that's a rhetorical question."

"You aren't curious?"

"Not in the least."

Daniel stared at the passing countryside. Sunlight streamed through the tall pines. He offered occasional navigational advice, but Lori must have memorized the map. She homed-in on 7645 Kelly Lane like a guided missile.

"Is this the level of seclusion you had in mind?" Lori asked.

Fisher's house sat back from the road at the end of a long tree-lined driveway. The nearest house was three hundred feet away, on the other side of a thick stand of trees.

"We won't have any nosy observers, that's for sure," Daniel answered.

He rolled down the car window. Fisher's home was a sprawling Colonial with a columned entrance portico.

"This really is a *huge* house," he said. "How many bedrooms do you figure?"

"At least six, maybe more. Look at all those second-story windows. And that has to be a four-car garage."

"It bewilders me that a widower would want so much space."

"Or a car that large," Lori said, and she maneuvered next to a long, top-of-the-line luxury car that was parked in front of the garage. "I wonder how it got here."

"I know the answer to that one. Rebecca Taylor told me that Tony paid the Glory Garage to tow it here from the marina. Of course, that was before he was charged with Fisher's murder."

Daniel climbed out of Lori's rental car and looked around. The police had tacked yellow Police Line—Do Not Cross tape across the wide garage doors and the front door. "I wonder when the cops will take the tape down," he said to Lori in a voice not much louder than a whisper.

She shrugged. "I doubt anyone's asked for it to be removed. In fact, I doubt anyone has been here since the police sealed the house. Rafe Neilson thinks that the house has passed to the executor of Quentin's estate."

"That would probably be his son, right?"

"I assume so.

Daniel moved closer to the house. The grounds were landscaped. The grass had been cut recently.

"Someone must be paying for lawn service," Lori said. "So we'll have to assume that the burglar alarm is also live." She pointed to a sign stuck in the ground near the entrance portico: This House Is Protected By Sentinel Security Of Elizabeth City.

"What kind of sensors are we up against?" Daniel asked.

"I'd say the usual collection of sensors you'd find in a well-protected home. Magnetic switches on windows and doors, plus a few motion detectors in large open areas. However..."

"What?"

"We probably should check for external TV cameras in weatherproof pods. They're usually mounted on the corners of a structure. You go left, I'll go right."

Daniel walked to the left side of the house. He wasn't sure what a "weatherproof pod" might look like, but there were no unexplained objects of any kind attached to the brick or wood trim. He found neatly cut firewood stacked in a metal rack that kept the logs off the ground, away from termites. A few steps beyond was a pile of paving bricks, the same color as the bricks used to build the house. Someone, probably Quentin Fisher, had begun to lay a brick pathway around the left side of the house. The route had been marked off by stakes and twine, and a ten-foot-long section of pathway had been completed.

Daniel returned to the front of the house. Lori was crouched on the driveway, next to her canvas tote bag.

"Ah...I get to look inside your bag of tricks," he said.

She held up a coil of silver wire about as thick as a drinking straw. "I call this gadget a snake camera," she said. "It's a long, flexible metal tube with a tiny TV camera in the tip. We can use it to inspect Quentin's house without opening any doors or windows."

Lori began to uncoil the "snake" on the driveway. "The metal tube is eight feet long." She glanced at him over her shoulder. "Please protect the lens on the end, I don't want it to get scratched by the driveway."

Daniel lifted the end of the long tube. The tiny glass

lens was rounded and dark gray in color, and looked like a miniature doll's eye. He took a step sideways as Lori sat cross-legged on the driveway. She booted up her laptop computer, then attached the cable that ran from the back of the snake. The lens began to glow brightly, except for a tiny area in the center.

"Did I mention that the camera has a built-in light source and will work in the dark?" Lori said.

"Nifty." He looked directly at the lens.

"Do you see your picture on the screen?" she asked.

Daniel leaned over. "Sort of."

"Put your mirrored shades on."

"I forgot."

Daniel found that the silvered lenses immediately improved the contrast of the picture on the laptop's screen. The image of his face was grainy but viewable, a lot better than one would think possible from such a small camera.

"Cool," he said.

He swung the tip of the snake around like a dueling sword and watched a kaleidoscope of jumbled pictures.

"If you're finished playing," Lori said, "we can go to work."

"Very funny." He stuck out his tongue. "What's our first subject?"

"The garage, of course. It should be easy to slide the snake underneath the soft weather stripping at the bottom of the doors." Lori uncurled her legs, lay on her stomach and fed the metal snake beneath the door. "I'll work the camera, you watch the screen and tell me what you see."

Daniel sat on the driveway and put the computer in his lap. "I see the inside of a big garage."

"Do you think you can be a tad more specific?"

"I think the camera is aimed at the back wall. I can see an impressive collection of gardening tools and a small tractor. It looks like enough equipment to operate a working farm."

"Push the Function Three key, near the top left of the keyboard."

"Okay. Can I ask what I just accomplished?"

"You captured a snapshot of the image on the screen. We'll look at it later to make certain that we didn't miss anything."

"Are you positive that we're not breaking and entering right now?"

"I believe that you have to physically enter a structure in North Carolina to be guilty of breaking and entering."

"*You believe*," Daniel said. "You aren't sure?"

Lori looked up at him. "I can't possibly know the law for every state I work in, now can I?"

"You're going to get us arrested!"

"Stop overreacting. We'll be finished in five minutes." She shifted position. "I'm moving the camera to the right."

"Well, I can see why Quentin Fisher needed such a large garage. There's an empty space where he must've parked his car and then there are two more vehicles. A red convertible—I guess that was his fun car—and a blue pickup."

"Make a snapshot."

"Way ahead of you." He added, "Move the camera a little more to the right."

"What do you see?"

"A door in the back of garage is open. It must be the laundry room—all I see is a washing machine and a dryer."

"You sound disappointed. What did you expect? A roomful of money?"

"Now that you mention it…" Daniel made another snapshot. "Where to now?"

Lori scrambled to her feet. "The back of the house. We'll take a look in his kitchen. I'll carry the snake, you bring the computer."

"Okay, but I don't think you'll be able to snake the snake past the back door."

"Not a problem."

Daniel spotted the reason for Lori's confidence as soon as they turned the corner. "There's a pet flap in the door," he said.

"For a pretty big dog, I'd guess. A German shepherd or a golden retriever."

Daniel looked around the backyard. "I haven't heard any barking. If there was a dog in the house, we'd have been barked at by now."

"Not if our theory is correct."

"What did he do with the dog—put it in a kennel?"

"More likely, he left it with his son on Long Island."

Lori knelt on the small raised porch in front of the door and pushed the snake camera through the flap. Daniel cradled the computer in his arms and looked at the screen.

"I see a typical, fancy kitchen," he said. "Big, with an island in the center."

"I'll try to aim the camera upward."

"Okay. Now I see a countertop. There's a microwave oven and a coffee machine, nothing else—no open boxes, no abandoned sticks of butter."

"Of course not. Quentin left the place clean because he didn't expect to come home again."

"You want me to take a snapshot?"

"Might as well. Then we'll move on."

Daniel helped Lori stand. "Now what?"

"I'm going to need your help to peek into windows. The house is built on a crawlspace, so I'll need something to stand on."

"Something to stand on…" Daniel muttered. "How about one of those Adirondack chairs on the patio?"

"Perfect!" She batted her eyelashes. "Now all we need is a big, strong man to carry it over here."

Daniel regretted his suggestion the moment he lifted the awkward-shaped lounge chair. It weighed at least sixty pounds and was difficult to carry. He and Lori repositioned the chair under four different windows until she said, "This is it—Quentin's home office. The window is heavily draped, but the drapes aren't completely closed. "I can see the edge of a desk. Can you hand me my canvas tote bag?"

"Here it is. What happens now?"

"This." She reached into the bag and brought out a small battery-operated drill.

"You're going to drill a hole!" Daniel knew that he'd shrieked rather than spoken the question.

"A insignificant small one. Just big enough for the snake."

Daniel groaned when she pressed the whirling drill bit against the window's wooden bottom rail. "That can't be legal."

"I intend to patch the hole when we're finished. Anyway—do you see anyone else around?"

"What if you set off the burglar alarm?"

"Why worry now? There was a motion detector in the kitchen. The snake probably didn't set that one off."

"Probably didn't?"

"Well, there's always a chance that the alarm is

working in silent mode. We wouldn't know if the system called the cops."

"Thanks for sharing!"

"I'm through the bottom rail! Give me a second—okay, the camera is inside the house. What do you see?"

"My life flashing before me," Daniel said.

"Cute! I'll be more specific—what do you see on the screen?"

"I see a tall stack of cardboard cartons in the center of the room. The desk you saw has an absolutely clean desktop and the bookcase beyond it is empty. If I didn't know better, I'd say he was planning to move."

"Move? To where? Shoot several snapshots while I maneuver the snake around."

Lori withdrew the snake and handed it to Daniel. He held the device while Lori patched the small hole with wood putty.

"You think of everything," he said.

"I certainly hope so, kind sir."

"Can we leave now?"

"Not until we try the front door."

"Does 'try' mean drilling a hole in the door?"

"No, silly. The front door is made of steel. My little drill would never penetrate it."

"Thankfully."

"However…" she said, "the glass panels on either side of the door have wooden frames. I'll bet we can drill through one of them."

"I hate you."

"No you don't."

"Harrumph."

"What's wrong?"

"We'll be more visible standing on the portico."

Lori scooped up her equipment. "We won't stay long. I promise."

Daniel followed behind Lori, unhappy at every step that brought them closer to the front of the house. At last they climbed the three steps that led to the raised portico.

"I'll watch for police cars," he said.

"Good idea," Lori said. "I see a nice, thick area of wood about a foot to the left of the door frame. It should be a fine place to drill."

"Is another hole *really* necessary?"

She took a step.

Clink.

Daniel saw Lori freeze. She looked at him wide-eyed. "I think the sound came from under the floorboard I'm standing on."

"It did," Daniel agreed.

"I've heard that weird metallic noise before."

"Me, too."

She took a deep breath. "A booby-trap treadle switch."

"Could be."

"If that's what it is, I armed the device when I stepped on the floorboard."

He nodded. "Keep absolutely still until we figure this out."

"I'm not going anywhere, believe me." She laughed, but her laugh sounded suddenly hollow.

"Can you hand me the snake without shifting your weight? I'll use the camera to see what you're standing on. Assuming of course that I can move freely."

"And how exactly will you determine that?"

"By moving freely."

She managed a smile, but Daniel could see fear in her eyes.

He went on, "If it's any consolation, I'm more frightened than you are."

"I doubt it. I *hate* things that go boom. That's why I didn't join the artillery."

"Here goes." Daniel took a step away from her. And then a step toward her. "Okay, I can move around. You're the one standing on the treadle—if that's what we're dealing with." He reached toward her. "Pass the snake to me."

Daniel didn't breath while Lori slowly extended her arm. He noted that her hand was trembling as he gently took the snake from her.

"You'll have hold the laptop steady while I feed the snake under the portico."

Daniel moved backward down the steps slowly, silently praying that the cable linking the snake to the computer was long enough to reach around the portico.

It was. *Praise the Lord.*

The side of the portico was solid except for a small ventilation panel covered with wire mesh. Daniel used his car key to punch a hole through the mesh, then fed the snake into the hole.

"Look at the screen," he called. "What do you see?"

"Wood studs, metal brackets, dirt…"

Daniel pushed the snake deeper under the portico and twisted the metal tube to elevate the tip. "What do you see now?"

"More wood and…*oh no!*"

Daniel raced to Lori's side and looked at the image on the laptop screen.

"We were right," she said between short, rapid breaths. "There's the treadle switch. It must be right under me."

"I don't see any explosives."

"No, but I see two wires—one red, one white—going off under the house."

Daniel returned to the side of the portico and yanked the snake out of the ventilation panel. He quickly looked around and found a small opening leading into the crawlspace under the house. He fed the snake into the opening.

"The camera is under the house now," he said. "What do you see?"

"Dirt, wood and the red-and-white wires."

He pushed the snake deeper into the crawlspace.

Lori began to shout. "I can see it! The wires lead to a package of explosives."

Daniel sprinted back up the steps.

"I don't get it," he said. "It looks like someone was trying to bomb Quentin Fisher. Doesn't that kill your theory?"

"What do you mean, my theory? You agreed with me." She swallowed hard. "Let's talk about it later."

"Listen," he said, touching her arm lightly. "We're okay as long as you keep standing still. I'll get help. There must be a bomb squad somewhere in this part of the state."

"You obviously nodded off during the second half of the explosives course. There's often a secondary timer that triggers after a certain number of minutes—even if the weight that armed the device isn't removed."

"Rats!"

"Enough with the expletives," Lori said evenly. "I'd like to hear a prayer out of you."

"A prayer?"

"Yeah. One of those speeches where you ask God for help, maybe even a miracle."

"I've been praying silently for the past half hour. I thought you preferred that God stayed out of your way."

"I might have given you that impression a few days ago, but circumstances change. Today I definitely want God to take center stage in my life."

"I'm shocked."

"Don't be. I've been thinking a lot about God lately."

"That's wonderful!"

"You were right about chatting with God. I've even begun to think of myself as a Christian again."

"You don't know how happy that makes me. In fact…"

"Save the small talk for later," Lori interrupted. "Pray about the treadle switch! And make it short."

"Good point." Daniel put his hand on Lori's shoulder. "Heavenly Father. We thank You for giving us warning of the peril we face. We ask for Your protection and Your wisdom to help us find a way out of the Valley of Death. Amen."

"Amen and Amen!" Lori said quickly. "Look, there's only one thing for you to do. You have to get off this portico. It's silly for both of us to be blown up."

"That's ridiculous. We need another idea."

"What's ridiculous about it? It's a perfectly sensible military command decision that will save as many lives as possible."

"I'm not going to leave you here."

"Why not?"

"Because I love you."

"You do?"

"Deeply and truly," Daniel said. He continued, "If there is a secondary timer, how long would it be set for?"

"It can be any reasonable length of time, I suppose. Why do you ask?"

"Because we probably want to finish this conversation at another time, in another place."

"Don't you want me to say that I love you?"

"Do you?"

"Lots! It would really be nice if you had another idea. A way to get both of us off this portico."

"Surprisingly, I do. We need to replace your weight on the floorboard with something of equal weight. How much do you weigh?"

"Let me think."

"About what?"

"Whether I'd rather get blown up than tell you what I weigh."

Daniel leaned forward and kissed her forehead.

"Why did you do that?" she asked.

"To cast my vote. I don't want you to get blown up. I really do love you."

"Oh, my." She sighed. "I think we need a recount." She tilted her face upward toward Daniel; he gently kissed her on the lips. She seemed to kiss him back, although the odd angle made it hard to be certain.

"I weigh one hundred and twenty-five pounds," she said, "give or take."

"That's a lovely weight. I'll be right back."

"And I'll be waiting here for you."

Daniel gingerly stepped off the portico again, praying this time for more wisdom, even better judgment and deliverance from the horrific danger they faced. He looked back at Lori, who was staring at the picture of the booby trap on the laptop screen. She seemed less nervous than before. And more beautiful than ever.

Concentrate on the booby trap. What can you use as a replacement weight?

Daniel's mind raced, considering and rejecting items around him. The Adirondack chair. The battery from the car. Firewood. And then he remembered the paving bricks.

He ran to the stack at the side of the house and hefted a brick in his hand. He estimated that it weighed about five pounds. Twenty-five bricks equaled one Lori—plus an extra brick for "give or take."

Daniel made a quick decision. Because bricks were awkward to carry, he would need four trips to carry the twenty-six bricks to the front of the house. He crooked his left arm and managed to stack seven bricks against his body, ignoring the pain caused by the sharp edges.

He half walked, half jogged to the portico and piled the bricks near the top of the three steps.

"You're pretty savvy for a pastor," Lori said. "Can I do anything to help? I feel useless just standing here."

"See if you can come up with a safe way to put the bricks where you're standing, without releasing any pressure on the floorboard."

Daniel carried seven more bricks during his second trip and six each during the third and fourth. He sat on the portico's steps to catch his breath when he finished.

"I hate to rush you," Lori said, "but I'm really eager to get off this stupid floorboard."

Daniel chuckled. "I see your point. Did you figure out how to get you off?"

"Build a stack of bricks, two bricks wide, two bricks

long, then push it slowly toward me. When the stack touches my shoes, I'll inch sideways—and you push some more."

"Maybe we should build a narrower stack—two bricks on the bottom rather than four. Your weight is concentrated on two feet."

She shook her head. "No. There's too much risk that a tall, narrow stack will topple over."

Daniel grunted in agreement and began to stack the bricks. He laid four bricks side to side, then placed the second layer crosswise to the first. He gave the eight-brick stack an experimental push and found that the bricks would slide against the varnished floorboards. He returned to laying bricks.

Daniel stood back and studied the finished stack. It was six layers high, with the twenty-fifth and twenty-sixth bricks sitting on the top. It seemed a stable and sturdy structure, unlikely to topple.

He began to push the bricks toward Lori.

Daniel had to sink to his knees as he moved the squat stack toward the interior of the portico. He found it difficult to brace himself for each new push. After perhaps thirty little shoves, the stack finally stood next to Lori's feet.

"Start inching," he said.

"That's a half inch," she replied.

He pushed the stack of bricks to take up the gap.

"Whoa!" she said. "Don't push me over."

"Sorry. Move another half inch."

"Done!"

"And another."

"Okay."

"And again."

"How many more?"

"At this rate, five or six."

"Should I pick up the pace."

"Nope. Slow and steady is usually better around bombs."

"Very droll."

"I try. Now, move again."

"The floorboard just creaked— Did you hear it, too?"

"I heard it. I think it means that were adding weight to the right spot."

"Should I move again."

"Why not?"

"Oops. Was that too far?"

"Apparently not." He glanced up at her. "As soon as my heart stops thumping, you can try again."

"If you think this is easy, you have a go."

Daniel tapped Lori's ankle. "Shift once more."

"My pleasure."

"Hmm."

"What does *that* mean?"

"I think we're there. The bricks are over the treadle switch, your feet are on the adjacent floorboard."

"Are you sure?"

"Reasonably." He stood. "But there's only one way to find out. You'll have to take a giant step to your right."

"Oh, boy! I knew that I wasn't going to like this part. Where will you be?"

"Right next to you."

"I'd like another kiss first."

"If you insist." Daniel carefully moved around Lori and kissed her again. This kiss left no doubt: she did kiss him back.

"I'm ready," she said, her voice quivering.

"One! Two! Three! *Move!*"

Lori leaped sideways and landed heavily on her right foot. Daniel felt the whole portico shake. He looked at the stack of bricks. Solidly in place.

"Praise God," she said.

"Let's get out of here," he shouted.

Daniel took Lori's arm and propelled her ahead of him down the steps. They ran along the driveway and took cover behind a robust oak tree about a hundred feet from the house. He put his arms around her and held her tightly.

"Nothing went bang," he said. "We fooled the treadle switch." He began to laugh with relief.

He felt Lori began to sob. "Don't mind me," she said with a long sniff. "I always cry when I'm happy."

He stroked her hair and kissed her again.

"I have to excuse myself for a moment," he said as he unwrapped his arms and took a step backward, feeling strangely wobbly.

Thank You, Lord. I'm grateful that we're both okay. I asked You to "encourage" Lori to seek You, but frankly I didn't expect You to arrange such a spectacular reunion.

"What's the matter, Daniel?" Lori peered at him quizzically.

"Nothing much. I have to throw up."

FOURTEEN

"I have tea, coffee and hot cocoa. What would you like?"

Emma Neilson set the large tray down on the coffee table in The Scottish Captain's front parlor, then added, "The homemade chocolate-shortbread cookies are especially delicious today, if I say so myself."

Not one of the three other people in the room responded. They all seemed lost in thought.

Emma wondered if she should ring a bell. It was understandable that Daniel Hartman and Lori Dorsett would be a bit spacey this evening. They were sitting together on a sofa, Daniel's arm firmly around Lori's shoulders. They needed time to recover from their frightening ordeal and—Emma chuckled to herself—begin to understand the new bond they'd obviously established. The pair looked right together, and seemed equally matched, two factors that Emma considered solid predictors of a good relationship.

But why was Rafe acting so reticent?

"Earth to Rafe Neilson," she said.

Emma was surprised when Daniel spoke first.

"You know, Lori and I were talking about that very subject the other day—about how things are not what they seem."

"Perhaps…but I get paid for not falling into that trap," Rafe said unhappily. "You can understand why I feel foolish. I also owe Tony Taylor more than an apology. I can't give him back the days he spent in jail."

So that's the problem, Emma thought. The poor baby is blaming himself for arresting Tony.

Emma spoke. "Tony will be home soon—with all the charges against him dropped. That's what really matters."

"I suppose you're right." Rafe looked up and smiled awkwardly. "I'll make sure that the district attorney files the papers first thing tomorrow morning. Tony will be singing with the choir on Sunday. Still, I feel like a world-class dolt. Lori saw things at the Glory at Sea Marina that I should have seen."

"I hate to speak ill of the dead," Lori said, "but I don't understand the evil things Quentin Fisher did. I've tried to imagine the world through his eyes, but I can't do it."

"I have to admit," Rafe said, "that the only thing I understand about this case right now is that Quentin Fisher killed himself."

Daniel sighed. "It's incredible."

"But true," Rafe said. "The papers we found in Fisher's house include a receipt for two garage-door transmitters and one receiver, and a circuit diagram for the battery-powered detonator we found in what was left of *Marzipan*. Rafe shook his head sadly. "Fisher caused the explosion aboard *Marzipan*, but he did it in a way that would make everyone think that Tony murdered him. For some bizarre reason, he wanted to end Tony's life along with his."

Lori chimed in. "He broke into Tony's office, hid one of the transmitters, sent the invitation e-mail to himself using Tony's computer and faxed the map using Tony's fax machine."

"Do we presume that he killed himself because he was seriously ill?" Emma said.

Rafe stared at her, she felt, with the concentrated focus of a laser beam. "Sorry, Emma, once burned, twice shy. I no longer assume anything about Quentin Fisher. We now know that he had inoperable pancreatic cancer. We found the diagnosis among his papers. By committing suicide, he accelerated the inevitable by six or seven months. He's certainly not the first person to do that. But it seems much too simple an explanation for the way he killed himself."

"I agree," Lori said. "If he just wanted to commit suicide, why go through the complex charade? He jumped through hoops to make his death look like murder. And he put other lives in danger with a booby trap."

Daniel nodded. "It was fortunate that no one else stepped on that treadle switch first. A policeman, a mailman, a distant relative, a delivery person, his defense attorney, a neighborhood child—anyone could have set off the explosive charge." Daniel frowned. "Fisher must have been a thoroughly demented person. I see no other explanation."

"I have to disagree, Daniel," Lori said. "I consider Quentin Fisher reckless, strong-minded and treacherous—but not demented. He was exceedingly clever. His plan almost worked perfectly. If someone—probably a policeman—had stepped on that treadle switch two weeks ago, the authorities would be running in all directions, not sure who killed Quentin Fisher—or why." Lori seemed to relax. "The only kind thing I can say about him is that he *didn't* set a secondary timer on the booby trap."

Emma waited for someone to keep the discussion

going. When no one did, she said, "I'll ask once again,"
Emma said. "Would you all like tea, coffee or hot cocoa?"

Rafe started to reach for a mug full of cocoa. He
stopped in midmotion and spoke to Lori. "Do you agree
with me that the real purpose of the blast was to destroy
his financial and account documents?"

"Absolutely," Lori said.

"Why blow up a bunch of paperwork?" Daniel asked.
"Why not just use a shredder?"

Lori patted his hand. "Because Fisher wanted the
police to find a mountain of debris and ashes, so it would
look like someone else destroyed his papers."

"I hate to keep asking why," Daniel said, "but *why*?"

"I don't know, but we have to find out."

"We do?" Daniel said. "Uh…*why*?"

"Because the investment waters are still muddy," Lori
said. "If we don't get a handle on Quentin Fisher's
motives, we'll have to fight McKinley Investments and
Chicago Financial Insurance every step of the way to get
the church's money back."

"The money," Daniel said with another one of his deep
sighs. "I keep forgetting about the money." He glanced
at Rafe. "I don't suppose that the police found any of the
church's money in Fisher's house."

"No such luck," Rafe said. "But we intend to keep
looking. Although, I'm not optimistic. A financial whiz
like Quentin Fisher doesn't have to bury money—he
knows how to hide it in banks and institutions."

"Banks and institutions create paper trails," Lori said.

"Indeed they do," Rafe said with a smile. "That's why
this stack of papers is sitting on the floor next to my re-
clining chair. These are copies of Quentin Fisher's

account documents that we found in his office. Next
week, I intend to go through them carefully. If somebody
were to borrow them until then, I probably wouldn't
notice that they were missing."

Emma sat back in her own chair and watched the other
three begin to laugh. No one seemed in the mood for tea,
coffee or cocoa.

Oh, well. More for me.

She reached for a chocolate-shortbread cookie.

Glory, North Carolina, seemed different to Lori on
Thursday morning. It began at The Scottish Captain,
when she felt certain that Emma Neilson served her an
extra-large portion of the inn's fabulous breakfast quiche.
And then, as she walked to Glory Community Church,
people who hadn't smiled at her in days went out of their
way to say, "Good morning."

Most amazing of all, when Lori arrived at the church,
Ann Trask leaped out of her chair and thrust a mug of
coffee into Lori's hands.

Apparently the same citizens of Glory who had been
furious with her were now willing to forgive her even
more rapidly—once they discovered that she really was
on their side.

Ann beamed at her. "Daniel, Christine and George are
meeting in the Adult Christian Education Classroom."
Ann leaned close to Lori and whispered, "Daniel has set
it up as a war room."

"Thank you," Lori said, "I don't want to be late."

"Oh, there's no hurry. They've been meeting since nine."

"Nine?" Lori tried to remember what Daniel had told
her the night before. "I thought the meeting began at ten?"

"Daniel wanted to make sure you got a good night's sleep after your experience yesterday." Ann lowered her voice to a whisper. "You'll find out that Daniel is exceptionally thoughtful that way."

"Um…yes…well, thank you again."

But Ann wouldn't let her go. "Fabulous things are happening as a result of what you and Daniel did yesterday. Tony Taylor is coming home this morning, did you know?"

"No, I hadn't heard."

"It's official! The state is dropping all charges against Tony. Tony's lawyer is on his way to the Albemarle District Jail to pick him up."

"That's wonderful news."

Lori tried again to leave, but Ann grabbed her wrist. "You can't go yet." Ann pressed a speed-dial button on her telephone, then activated the speakerphone feature.

"Good morning," a woman's voice said. "This is Rebecca Taylor."

"Hi, Rebecca," Ann said. "As promised, Lori is standing next to the telephone. I've got you on speaker."

"Hello, Lori," Rebecca said. "I heard what you did for Tony, and I wanted to thank you. Ann told me that you will be working on church business this morning, so this is the best way to do it." Lori heard Rebecca swallow a sob. "You and Daniel gave Tony his life back. I don't know how we can ever thank you."

"I'm looking forward to finally meeting Tony."

Rebecca began to sob and Lori felt tears welling. She noted that Ann Trask was dabbing her eyes with a tissue.

"Yes," Rebecca said with a sniff. "I intend to throw Tony a doozy of a welcome-home party. Naturally, you and Daniel are invited."

"Thank you, Rebecca. We'll be there."

You and Daniel—that was another phrase that seemed to be on people's lips this morning. From Ann Trask, to Emma Neilson, to Rebecca Taylor, the townsfolk of Glory seemed to acknowledge that Lori Dorsett and Daniel Hartman had fallen for each other.

"Should I do it now?" Ann said—to the telephone.

"Please do," Rebecca replied.

Ann abruptly gave Lori a tight hug.

Rebecca's voice came from the speaker, "Consider that from me."

Lori noted that the classroom had been rearranged since she'd last seen it. The room was equipped with six rectangular tables that could each accommodate three students. Someone—probably Daniel—had pushed the tables together to create one large "conference table" in the middle of the room. Someone else—Ann Trask, Lori guessed—had cleaned the three chalkboards in the room.

I will never again betray my friends.

Lori pictured the hundreds of words she'd written. She realized that they had taken root in her psyche. There would be no more undercover assignments, no more deception, no more lying.

Each of the Big Three had staked out one side of the table: Daniel to the east, Christine to the north, George to the west. They had left the south side for her. The stack of papers that Rafe had lent them sat on the southeast corner, in easy reach of Daniel and herself.

"Good morning!" Daniel rose to greet her. He gave her a quick kiss on the cheek.

"Good morning," she replied, her heart pleasantly fluttery.

George, busy drawing doodles on a yellow legal pad, smiled wistfully at her. She returned a wink. He suddenly seemed embarrassed and returned to his doodling.

Daniel pointed to a built-in shelf at the side of the room. "I made coffee and tea."

Christine added, "And Emma Neilson positively insisted that I bring that bag of cookies."

"Let me open this meeting in prayer," Daniel said. "Heavenly Father, we thank You that the fog is beginning to clear. We praise You for revealing the information that brought Tony Taylor's freedom. We ask that You grant us insight and discernment as we strive to penetrate the mystery of Glory Community's lost resources. In Your Son's name we pray."

Daniel smiled at Lori. "Well, what should we do first?"

Lori felt a tremor of surprise as she realized the others expected her to take charge of this meeting. She wished that she hadn't been as confident the day before, but she hadn't made promises she might not be able to keep.

Lori reached over to the stack of papers, picked up the top document and examined it. It appeared to be a copy of a typical account statement sent monthly by McKinley Investments. She dropped it back on the pile. Were these documents really going to tell them where the church's money had gone?

"My thoughts exactly!" Christine had apparently read Lori's gloomy expression. But her voice was enthusiastic, almost cheerful. "However…" Christine began to smile. "Our in-house financial wizard, George, figured out Fisher's scam this morning."

Lori couldn't help smiling, too. George deserved a chance to restore his reputation. He appeared eager to give a lecture on the topic. Well, anyone who decoded Fisher's convoluted scheme was entitled to gloat a little.

"Do your thing, George," Lori said. "Tell me what you learned."

George cleared his throat. "There are more than one hundred account documents in that pile. Twenty-seven of them are addressed to a box number—including ours. I sorted the pile this morning—the box number addresses are on top of the pile."

George obviously wanted Lori to ask for an explanation, so she obliged him. "Why would that be, George?"

"That's how Fisher intercepted the statements. He had them sent to box numbers and then forged his own statements, which he sent to account owners." George waved a piece of paper, then went on. "Here's the church's real statement. We know why he faked our account statement. The real statement shows that our deposits never reached McKinley Investments."

George looked hopefully at Lori again. "That of course raises an interesting question: Why did Fisher have to send these other twenty-six investors phony account statements?"

An idea bloomed in Lori's mind. "Stealing our money was only half of Quentin Fisher's challenge. He also wanted to make it disappear."

George beamed at Lori. "Precisely! He laundered the cash he stole from us through the other twenty-six accounts. The actions he took appear on the real statements, that's why he couldn't let them be sent to the account holders."

"And you figured out what Quentin Fisher did?"

"In three minutes flat," Christine said merrily.

George gave a disparaging wave. "It wasn't very hard. All I had to do was to look at those twenty-six documents. They have something obvious in common."

Lori stood and moved to the corner of the table. She began to examine the account statements. She caught on by the eighth statement. "Every person has invested in gold."

"Not just gold," George said, "but gold coins minted in Canada—the Canadian Gold Maple Leaf. Each coin is one ounce of pure 24-karat gold. They're very easy to buy and sell because the coins are official currency and are guaranteed by the Government of Canada for weight and purity."

"You're telling me that all twenty-six investors bought Gold Maple Leaf coins?" Lori asked.

"That's the tip-off," George said. "Gold can be a fine investment—for certain kinds of investors. But you wouldn't expect such a broad cross-section of small-town people to buy gold coins."

Lori nodded slowly. "I get it! He laundered the church money by converting it into gold coins. The man was a twisted genius."

Daniel threw up his hands. "Then I must be an untwisted dunce. I still haven't grasped what Quentin Fisher did, or how buying gold coins enabled him to make our money disappear." He looked pleadingly at Lori. "Christine seems to understand what Fisher did and George has tried to explain it to me *twice*. Since you obviously to get it, will you please clue me in?"

"I'll try." She winked at George. "Let's work together to see if we can put together an explanation that even a pastor will understand."

Lori picked up the topmost account statements again. "This document is addressed to a Mrs. Janice Bradley in

Edenton. She owns a tidy nest egg that includes several mutual funds, three blocks of shares in major corporations, another block of shares in an electric utility, and fifty Canadian Gold Maple Leaf coins."

George took over. "Except…Mrs. Bradley knows nothing about the gold. She never bought any."

"Who did buy it?" Daniel asked.

"Quentin Fisher," George said, "using the money he stole from the church."

Lori waved the document. "A month later, McKinley Investments sent this account statement to Mrs. Bradley. Naturally, Quentin didn't want her to see it, so he intercepted the real document, like he did the others, and mailed her a phony statement that doesn't list the gold coins as one of her assets."

"Where is the gold?" Daniel asked.

"The coins *were* in a vault operated by McKinley Investments," Lori said.

"What do you mean, 'were' in a vault?"

George jumped back in. "Lots of investors like to hold gold coins themselves. Why not? They're pretty to look at. Fisher probably sent a counterfeit request from Mrs. Bradley asking that the coins be delivered to her account representative—Quentin Fisher—so that he could pass them on to her."

"Tah-dah!" Lori said with a flourish-like gesture. "Fisher now has the gold coins, our money is gone for good, and the so-called investment no longer shows up on Mrs. Bradley's account statement."

George finished the explanation. "So now, Fisher can stop sending her phony statements. Everything is back to normal—except our bank account."

"George Ingles, you are a *genius*," Lori said. She planted a fat, friendly kiss on George's cheek. He began to blush uncontrollably.

"We can't explain it any clearer than that, Daniel," Lori said.

Daniel gave a begrudging nod. "Okay, I understand what Fisher did. But what happened to the gold?"

"That's the point," George said. "Fisher has it."

"No he doesn't," Daniel said. "At least, the gold's not in or near his house. The police searched the place—we'd have heard had they'd discovered a million-dollar hoard of Canadian gold coins."

Lori felt her heart skip a beat. Gold coins were the most portable of assets, a form of wealth that could be disposed of anywhere in the world. Quentin might have converted the coins into currency overseas. He might have hidden them in a safe-deposit box that no one else knew about. He might have even buried them in a distant corner of his property.

Lori sank despondently into her chair, her optimism quickly fading. They might never find the coins, leaving the church the uncertain option of continuing the lawsuit against McKinley Investments—which might now drag on for years.

Lori abruptly realized that Christine was trying to get her attention. "Your handbag is ringing," Christine said.

Lori recognized the distinctive ring tone of her satellite telephone. She picked up her handbag. "I'd better take this call. I'll be back as quick as I can."

The phone went silent after five rings. By the time she'd walked to the library alcove and positioned herself next to the window, the voice mail icon was lit. No need to retrieve the message; Kevin wanted to speak to her—immediately.

She dialed his number.

"Where are you?" he said gruffly.

"In Glory, North Carolina."

"Unsatisfactory. Return to Chicago on the next available flight."

"I can't do that."

"If you want to keep working for me, you will."

"I'm sorry, Kevin, but I've begun something in Glory that I intend to see through."

"No matter what I say?"

"No matter what you say."

"In that case, Lori, I say…you're fired!"

Click.

"Goodbye to you, too, Kevin," Lori said to the dead telephone.

Lori returned to the classroom, retook her seat and commenced to stare at the table.

"Do you want to talk about it?" Daniel asked.

Lori lifted her eyes and discovered that Christine and George had silently left the room. She was alone with Daniel.

"I've seen that look of confusion and anger on many faces," he said.

"My boss fired me," she said softly.

"How do you feel?"

"Scared, mostly—I've never been fired before. And angry at Kevin for losing his patience with me. And I guess a touch excited. This is my chance to find a job that doesn't require me to forever deceive people. Now that I'm a Christian again, that seems important to me."

"Amen!" Daniel said. "This breaks your ties to Chicago."

"So it does," she replied.

"We haven't talked about that yet."

"No we haven't," she said. "That's another scary topic."

Daniel touched her cheek. "You could become a North Carolina travel photographer."

She groaned. "Too true! I took two photos of everything worth photographing in Glory." She added, "Fortunately, they all belong to my former employer. I shot them in the line of duty."

"Fortunately?"

"The truth is, I found all that picture-taking a drag."

"Then maybe Glory needs another cop. That would be a way of using your CID training."

"I'm not sure that I'm cut out for small-town policing."

"I didn't think I was cut out for small-town pastoring—but I've never been happier."

"Let's make big decisions later. Right now, I need a hug."

Daniel took Lori in his arms and kissed her forehead. "Do you feel better?"

"Much." She broke free of his embrace. "We'd better get back to work."

"That's our cue," Christine said as she led George back into the room."

"You waited just outside the door?" Lori asked.

"Of course—we didn't think it proper to listen through walls like you did."

Lori rolled her eyes dramatically. "There's no privacy in a small town."

"You got that right!" George said.

Lori laughed along with everyone else.

Lori and the Big Three ordered a pizza from the Glory Pizza Pro restaurant.

Lori was trying to maneuver an especially cheesy slice of sausage pizza when Daniel said, "Guys, I still don't understand why a financial professional like Quentin Fisher had to go to all the trouble to transform our money into gold coins. Why didn't he just keep the cash in a shoe box? Why did he have to dry clean it?"

"The term is 'launder,'" George said. "By laundering the money, he could use it without fear that it might later be traced and identified as stolen."

"Hold it, George," Christine said. "Daniel makes an interesting point. Fisher probably had lots of quick and easy ways to launder our investment bucks. Why did he decide to make twenty-six different straw purchases of Canadian Maple Leaf coins?" She turned to Lori. "Did you ever do a deep database search on Quentin Fisher—the same kind of hunt your company did on George?"

"Nope," Lori said. "And it's obviously too late to ask."

"Well, I still have access to Lexis/Nexis," Christine said. "I'm not a great online researcher, but let's see what I can find. Where's the nearest computer with Internet access?"

"In my office," Daniel said. "Have at it."

Christine came back scarcely twenty minutes later, an enormous grin on her face.

"I'm not sure what all of it means," Christine said, "but there's a strange connection between Quentin Fisher and gold coins. His son, Will Fisher, the fellow who lives on Long Island, works for Kemany Brothers, a leading gold-coin broker in New York City." She paused an instant. "Guess what kind of gold coins they consider their specialty?"

"The Canadian Maple Leaf?" Lori said.

"Bingo!" Christine sat at the table. "Now here's the

really interesting part. Two weeks ago, Kemany issued a news release announcing that Will, who is thirty-three and a graduate of the Harvard Business School, is currently on administrative leave while the firm's auditors examine 'irregularities' in his accounts."

"How does that tie to what his father did to us?" Daniel asked.

Lori stood slowly. "I think I can explain everything that Quentin Fisher did. It all makes perfect sense—if you keep reminding yourself that things aren't always what they seem."

FIFTEEN

Daniel's eyes abruptly popped open. He read the glowing dial on his alarm clock. Three fifty-nine. To his great satisfaction, his brain had known the time without the help of an external clock and had awakened on its own. He still possessed a talent he had nurtured when most of his days began at Oh-Dark-Thirty.

He hit the clock's off button and spoke his first prayer of the morning. "Lord, You made this day and I am thankful for it. If it is Your wish, this will be the day that saves Your church. Lord, I place my concerns in Your hands knowing that what happens to Glory Community Church is Yours to decide. Help me accept Your will in all things. Amen."

Daniel climbed out of bed wondering if Lori had ignored her alarm clock. He considered calling her to make sure she was awake, but decided that would be foolish. She had just as much experience living by a military clock as he did. He felt confident they would both be early for their scheduled five o'clock departure time.

It had been Christine Stanton who had proposed an impromptu visit to Will Fisher.

"We know that he's home today," she had said. "I dialed his number on my cell phone and a young man answered. I pretended I'd reached a wrong number. Let's assume he'll also be home tomorrow and pay him an un-announced visit."

"Just show up on his doorstep, you mean?" Daniel had said.

"Will Fisher is smart, he's in trouble, and he's under no obligation to see us. Why give him a chance to pretend to be out when we show up?"

"Let's not forget that he recently lost his father. Is it really necessary to intrude on his grief?"

"A brief visit to inquire about a stash of gold coins isn't much of an intrusion."

Lori had asked, "Do you think he has the gold?"

"He has the coins—or he knows where they are," Christine said. "I feel it in my gut."

"Who makes the trip?" Daniel asked.

"You and Lori, of course," Christine said. "That's a no-brainer. You speak for Glory Community Church. Lori speaks for the companies that will eventually make good for Quentin Fisher's illegal actions."

Daniel had looked at Lori. "What do you think?"

"I think it's worth a try," she had said. "Where on Long Island does Will Fisher live?"

Daniel had stood behind George Ingles while he used a computer mapping program to search for the town of Stony Brook, in Suffolk County. Everyone agreed that it would be possible to make a one-day trip to visit Will Fisher, if…

If Lori and I get up in the middle of the night.

Daniel showered, dressed quickly, dashed downstairs

and nuked a mug of coffee. As he watched the mug revolve in his microwave oven, he wondered if the coffee was one day or two days old.

When the chime sounded he tasted the ancient brew and emptied the mug in the sink.

There's Lori to think of this morning. I'll make a fresh pot.

Thirty minutes later, at four fifty-five, he spotted Lori sitting in a rocking chair on The Scottish Captain's wide front porch. She jumped to her feet when she saw his car rolling along Broad Street.

Daniel noted that she wore a pair of tan slacks and the blue blazer that made her look especially shapely.

Lori slid into the passenger seat. For a moment Daniel felt overwhelmed by her flowery perfume. He fought hard not to sneeze.

Lori chuckled. "I can see by the asphyxiated look on your face that I overdid the eau de cologne this morning. It's hard to know how much to splash when you're half asleep." She chuckled. "I thought these middle-of-the-night missions were over when I left the Army."

"Did you sleep well?" he asked.

"Not especially. Truth be told, I feel nervous about today."

"Why? You seem to have solved the mystery. You know why Quentin Fisher did what he did." He pulled away from the curb. "Even though you refuse to share your theory with the rest of us."

"There's a chance that I'm wrong."

"A big chance?"

"Of course not." She chortled. "How did you sleep last night?"

"Pretty good, considering. I'm nervous, too, but this

morning I decided to place everything in the Lord's big hands."

"That's a nice sentiment, Daniel. But is it really possible to give your troubles to Jesus?" She shook her head. "That strikes me as a tad irresponsible."

"Give it a try, and you'll discover that turning your problems over to Jesus is the most responsible thing you can do. But it's difficult to learn to trust God. My biggest faith challenge is remembering not to take my problems back from the Lord." He hoped that his words didn't sound pompous or patronizing. He had to remember that Lori was working out her faith on her own terms.

"Whatever." She looked down into the passenger foot well. "Hey! Is that thermos full?"

"Freshly brewed coffee. Help yourself."

"Bless you. The breakfast coffee at The Captain won't be ready for at least another hour and the pod machine is on the fritz." She went on, grimly. "I can be a monster in the morning until I've had my coffee. Be afraid. Be very afraid."

"I also heated a couple of breakfast burritos to eat along the way." He crooked his thumb and pointed behind him. "Check the plastic insulated bag on the rear seat. We don't have time to stop on the way to the airport."

"I forget. What is our schedule?"

"We have an eight o'clock flight out of Norfolk International Airport, which is seventy-two miles from Glory."

"Do you realize," she said, "that this is the third or fourth time I've set sail for Norfolk in the past few days. Only this time I'm not returning to Chicago, but traveling to Long Island via Philadelphia. Now how strange is that?"

He reached behind his seat with his right hand and helped Lori heft the insulated bag to the front of the car.

If her original travel plans had worked, she'd be back in her office thinking about her next undercover assignment. The thought made him shiver.

"You don't appear to be overly concerned about your, ah…current employment situation," Daniel said.

"Actually, I can be a lady of leisure for a while. I looked up my employee's manual last night. Chicago Financial Insurance owes me twelve weeks of severance and another three weeks of paid vacation."

He glanced at Lori. She had unzipped the insulated bag and had partially unwrapped the two burritos. A moment later she gave him one and began to nibble on the second.

"While we eat breakfast," he said, "I'd like to talk about the elephant riding in the back seat."

"Uh…*o-kay*," she said after a short hesitation. Her voice sounded cautious, her tone on guard. Daniel understood; he could feel his own heart knocking against his chest.

"I love you and you love me," he said. "You are presently jobless in North Carolina, which gives you a perfect opportunity *not* to return to Chicago."

"Are you suggesting that I take up residence in Glory?"

"Secondarily."

"Pardon me?"

"My primary suggestion is that you marry me."

He heard her gasp and then cough several times.

"Are you okay?"

"Here's a safety hint. Never, ever propose marriage to a woman while she's eating a breakfast burrito." She coughed again. "Excuse me while I sip some coffee and clear my windpipe."

Daniel kept his eyes fixed on the road and began to eat his own burrito. Had he had made a strategic blunder by speaking so directly? Well, what were his choices? He'd risked frightening her away by speaking his mind, but if he said nothing, she might soon be on her way back to Chicago.

Lori broke the silence. "I hear your elephant braying, so let's talk more about why he's riding with us. He's really asking, How can I marry a pastor? Or more to the point, How can a pastor marry me?"

"We both say 'I do,' in the usual kind of ceremony."

"And then what?"

Daniel saw, in his peripheral vision, a hand holding a half-eaten breakfast burrito move in a sweeping gesture.

She began talking again. "We have to face facts, Daniel. I know how to plant electronic surveillance bugs. I'm a pretty good shot with a standard-issue Beretta 9mm automatic. I still remember most of my hand-to-combat training. And I know how to organize an effective stakeout. On the other hand, I can't bake cookies, I don't know the right way to host an afternoon tea, and I'd be terrified comforting someone who's just lost a spouse."

"Ah. You think you don't know how to be a small-town pastor's wife."

"Correct. I was trained to be an investigator." She twisted in her seat to face him.

"And I was trained to be an Army chaplain," Daniel said. "I knew almost nothing about being a small-town pastor when I arrived in Glory. I learned quickly—on the job. With God's help, so will you."

"Aren't there rules against pastors marrying women who haven't been inside a church for twenty-four years?"

"I don't recall discussing that particular topic at seminary."

"Stop trying to be funny, Daniel. You know exactly what I mean."

"Yes I do. That's one of the things that makes Grace so amazing. You can restore your relationship with God instantly."

"Even someone who lied for a living?"

"As far as God's concerned."

He felt the seconds ticking by and knew that Lori was staring at him.

What more could he say that might convince her to stay in Glory, to realize that she'd been forgiven, to marry him? *Lord, help me out here.*

Daniel found the quiet in the car oppressive, but his mind felt strangely empty. All he could do was to wait for Lori to talk.

"Okay," she suddenly said. "God seems to want me to marry you, so I will. But don't blame me if I'm the worst pastor's wife in the history of Christendom."

Daniel trod on the brake pedal and brought the car to a dusty stop on the shoulder of the road.

"You *will* marry me?" he said.

"I'm afraid so."

"Do I get to kiss my fiancée?"

"Hmm. You do realize that we both have burrito breath?"

"That seems to be the least of our challenges."

Daniel unclipped his seat belt and slid toward Lori.

"Passengers on Flight 8734 to Philadelphia proceed to gate seven."

Daniel put his arm around Lori's shoulder. "That's us."

She shook herself loose. "There's something else you don't know about me, Daniel. I *hate* to fly."

"How is that possible? Didn't your job as an under-cover investigator require you to fly all over the country?"

"I loathed every second in the air." After a pause she said, "I'm going to have to hold your hand."

She reached over, grasped his fingers and stepped aboard, all the while looking green around the gills. Her grip tightened as they took their seats.

"Hold," Daniel discovered, was a euphemism. Within seconds after the plane began to taxi, she had gripped his hand with the power of a five-fingered wrench. Lori squeezed the blood out of his fingers when the small jet began to accelerate on the runway. The digital pressure increased on the second leg of their trip.

When Lori glanced out the window and saw the Atlantic Ocean, she grimaced and said, "I hate flying over water most of all."

"You could try giving your worries over to God."

Lori laughed.

Soon after, Daniel noticed, Lori fell asleep. He tried to join her, but couldn't. Unhappy thoughts about lost gold coins kept him alert.

Sorry, Lord, I didn't mean to take my problem back— but it happened again.

He braced for the thump as the plane landed at MacArthur Airport.

"Are we here?" Lori asked with a yawn.

"In one piece and on time. Twelve-thirty to be exact."

Daniel and Lori picked up a rental car at the kiosk. Once seated inside, he unfolded the map to Will's house that George had prepared the day before.

"Who needs a map?" Lori asked. "The car has a GPS navigator."

Daniel's heart fell. "It takes me forever to learn to work electronic systems."

"I'll have a go." Lori began punching the buttons. "We're here—" she touched her finger to the display "—just south of Ronkonkoma. It looks like Route 29 runs right to Stony Brook. It's less than a thirty-minute trip—even allowing for lots of traffic lights."

"That's not the route that George's mapping system chose."

"Yeah, but this one takes us past several restaurants. I'm famished. The breakfast burrito was great, but I finished it hours ago."

"You're going to be a high-maintenance wife."

"But of course!" She touched more buttons. "There's a promising-looking diner in Lake Grove. Follow the little arrow on the screen, Daniel."

The first sight of Will Fisher's house through the windshield of their rental convinced Daniel that stopping for lunch had been an excellent idea. At least they felt refreshed and awake.

Daniel guessed the two-story Colonial was more than fifty years old and that it hadn't been maintained during the last ten years. Its cedar-shake siding was badly weathered and black-stained in many places. The double-wide wooden garage door looked as if someone had recently backed a car into it. Some of the shutters were cracked and those that weren't needed a fresh coat of paint. And nearly all of the screens were torn. Daniel imagined that every mosquito on Long Island had probably dined on Will Fisher.

"This doesn't look like the house of a man who has a million dollars in gold coins," he said to Lori.

"Check out his wheels." Lori pointed to a two-seater convertible parked at the top of the crushed oyster-shell driveway.

"Nice car," Daniel said.

"I think we're in luck. Fisher is probably home."

Daniel scampered to keep up with Lori as she marched to the front door with fierce determination. She pressed the doorbell button. A chime ding-donged deep within the house.

"I hear someone coming to the door," she said.

Daniel moved forward as the door swung wide. He couldn't help gaping at the tall, slender man in a stained polo shirt, crumpled blue jeans and bare feet.

"William Fisher?" Daniel said.

The man squinted, then nodded. "Yeah. Will Fisher."

Fisher looked as though he hadn't slept in a week. He was bleary-eyed, unshaven and pasty-faced. His thinning, mousy-brown hair soared in all directions.

Daniel watched Fisher bring his right hand out from behind his back. Daniel felt a jolt of fear. There was a gun in Fisher's hand, pointing down at the ground.

Lori didn't hesitate. In one fluid motion, she gripped Fisher's wrist with her left hand and grabbed the top of the pistol with her right.

"Let me hold this for you," she said. "It looks like a very nice 9mm automatic." She slid the magazine out of the frame and worked the slide to remove the live cartridge in the chamber.

"What?" He blinked, then nodded. "Oh, the pistol. It was my father's gun. Trouble is, I didn't have the courage to shoot myself. I tried on the night I heard that my father was dead, but I couldn't make myself pull the trigger. Dad was the brave one in the family. I'm a useless coward."

Fisher peered at Daniel. "Who are you?"

"My name is Daniel Hartman. I'm the pastor of Glory Community Church, in Glory, North Carolina."

"Glory? Is that near Hertford and Elizabeth City?"

"Right down the road."

Will suddenly became alert. "Why are you here?"

Lori answered first. "We've come to talk about the gold coins, Will."

"What kind of gold coins?" Will said, almost belligerently.

"Canadian Gold Maple Leafs."

"Why should I know about gold coins?"

"Because Quentin Fisher, your father, gave you nearly a million dollars' worth of gold coins to replace the coins you embezzled from your employer."

Daniel felt himself gawking at Lori, but Fisher's face relaxed into a smile. "Praise the Lord. I hoped you'd come. I've been praying for you to come for weeks." He made a vague wave. "Well, ever since my father died."

"You expected us to visit you?" Lori said, clearly bewildered by Fisher's statement.

"Yes, I did." He looked at Lori intently. "By the way, who are you? And why did you take my pistol?"

Daniel answered the first question. "Will, let me introduce Lori Dorsett, my fiancée."

"Hello, Will," Lori said. "About the pistol—since you don't plan to shoot yourself, I took the cartridges out."

Fisher seemed lost in thought for several seconds before he nodded. "That's probably a good idea. Now that

you're here I don't need to guard the gold anymore." He
smiled at Lori. "Do you want to come in?"

"That would be lovely," she said.

Fisher stepped backward and beckoned Daniel and
Lori through the doorway with a tilt of his head.

Daniel followed Will and Lori into an unfurnished
foyer and living room. The hardwood floors were bare
and scuffed; the walls needed repainting.

"That's what you came for." Fisher pointed at a small
wheeled suitcase, its handle extended, that stood like a
lone sentry in the center of the living room. "Be careful
when you lift it. It weighs more than seventy pounds."

"May we look inside?" Lori said.

Fisher shrugged. "It's yours now. Do what you like."

Daniel watched while Lori carefully laid the heavy
suitcase on its back and unzipped the front panel. Inside
were dozens of clear plastic rectangles, each with a gleaming
gold coin inside. Lori lobbed one of the rectangles to Daniel.

George Ingles had been right: the Canadian Gold
Maple Leaf was a pretty coin indeed, a bit smaller than
an American fifty-cent piece, with a portrait of Queen
Elizabeth on one side and the maple leaf on the reverse.
Daniel lobbed the rectangle back to Lori.

"It's all there," Fisher said, "all the coins Dad gave
me. About nine hundred and fifty thousand dollars'
worth of gold."

"You seem to have been expecting us," Daniel said.
"How is that possible?"

"When I found out what my father had done, I prayed
that you would figure it out—and ask for your money back."

Lori zipped the suitcase shut. "Why didn't you call the
church and tell us you had the coins?"

"I didn't know who to call." He heaved a sigh. "My father didn't tell me who he had cheated. He didn't want me to know where the money came from."

Daniel moved close to Will. "When did you eat last?"

"The other day, I guess. There's plenty of food in the kitchen. I'm just not in the mood to cook it."

Daniel and Lori followed him into the kitchen. To Daniel's surprise, it was a relatively cheerful room that seemed fully furnished, with the usual array of appliances, a complete set of kitchen cabinets and a chromed-leg dinette set with a pink Formica top.

Daniel whispered in Lori's ear, "You seem to know what's going on—you do the inquisition, I'll prepare a meal for Will."

He looked in the refrigerator and the cabinets. Will had exaggerated about his food inventory, but Daniel found the makings of a reasonably good lunch: a package of macaroni and cheese, a can of Manhattan clam chowder and a box of oyster crackers. He began to cook, with one ear cocked toward Lori and Will, who had taken seats at the dinette table.

"Had you stolen money from Kameny Brothers before?" Lori asked.

"Small amounts, here and there."

"Can I ask why? You seem to have had an excellent job."

"Gambling. A heavy-duty addiction. It's like a demon—once it gets hold of you, you can't get free. At least, not without the right help."

"And your father had been bailing you out?" Lori said.

"Like clockwork. I would call him, he would send money." He made a sour face. "But that changed six months ago. I went on a binge. I lost almost a million dollars. The only way I could pay my gambling debt was by 'borrowing' gold coins from Kameny Brothers."

"You had no other assets?"

"My house and my car are mortgaged to the max."

"But this time, your father couldn't bail you out?"

"After I spoke to him," Will said, "I realized that he didn't have that much cash. His own investments weren't doing that well—he would've had to sell everything, including his house."

"But he did come up with the coins you needed?"

Will nodded. "He called me in January, said that he would soon take care of everything—but he had one requirement. I had to become a member of Gamblers Anonymous."

"Did you?"

"That's the funny thing. I'd joined GA two months earlier." Will shook his head as if to shake a thought loose. "In February, he brought me those gold coins. I've never seen Dad look worse—he seemed a tormented man. It took me about five minutes to figure out that he had stolen the money to save me."

"Did he tell you how he stole the funds?"

"He didn't have to. I know how brokerages work and I know all about the gold coin business. There aren't that many ways to steal money, given the protections that are in place today."

"But then something went wrong?"

Will peered at Lori. "Exactly! A man started asking the wrong kinds of questions."

Daniel glanced at Lori. She gave an almost imperceptible nod and mouthed, "Tony Taylor."

Will went on. "Dad became worried that his accounts

would be audited. We both knew that he'd left a paper trail that would enable a good investigator to figure out what he'd done." Will shut his eyes. "In February, Dad told me not to worry, that he had found a way to sever the links between him and the gold. It took me ten seconds to figure out the rest of his plan."

"Did you know your father was ill?"

"Yeah, but that doesn't make it right for him to commit suicide to save me."

"He did more than that. He made his suicide look like murder to muddy the waters, to confuse and confound anyone looking at his recent activities. He was even willing to sacrifice his house in Hertford—all to make sure that no one ever traced the gold to you."

Will slapped the table hard. "I begged Dad to take back the coins. I told him that when I joined Gamblers Anonymous I also rebuilt my relationship with Jesus, that I was okay with going to prison, that I wasn't going to return the coins to Kemany." He gave a thin laugh. "Dad told me I was being foolish, that I had my life ahead of me, while his was almost over."

"And then you heard that your father was dead?"

"First, I made the arrangements for his funeral. Second, I tried to shoot myself. When that didn't work, I began praying for you folks to come."

"You had the coins your father gave you, yet you never replaced the coins you 'borrowed' from Kemany. Why?"

"I couldn't bring myself to do it—not after my father killed himself. Two weeks ago, time ran out for me. They did an audit of my accounts. I'm toast," Will said cheerfully.

Daniel nearly dropped the bowl of soup he'd just prepared.

Daniel lifted the suitcase full of gold coins into the rental car's trunk. Will Fisher appeared almost ecstatic to see the treasure taken away from his home. Daniel felt a flood of compassion for the gaunt man standing next to him. Will seemed to be genuinely repentant, acutely aware of the pain he'd caused—and on the mend.

"Would you like me to pray for you before we leave?" Daniel asked. Will nodded; Daniel took his hands. "Lord, we all come before You as sinners. We break Your commandments and do things that displease You. Yet for reasons we can't understand You continue to forgive us and love us. Help our brother Will overcome his addiction and to live a life that is pleasing to You. And help Will to understand that he is not a useless coward—that he has incalculable worth because You love him, and that no coward would have chosen the course he did. We ask these things in Jesus' name. Amen."

Daniel opened his eyes in time to see two large tears roll down Will's face. Lori turned away quickly, but a sniff gave her away.

"Keep praying for me, Reverend Hartman," Will said. "I'd like that very much." He disappeared into the house without a backward glance.

Daniel slipped into the driver's seat. Lori spoke immediately. "You know, of course, that we can't check that suitcase at the airport. The security people would freak when their X-ray machine spotted a million dollars' worth of Canadian gold coins."

"You want to drive back to Glory?"

"Yep. According to the GPS navigator it's about four hundred and twenty miles from here to the Norfolk

Airport, where we can turn this car in and pick your car up. That's an eight-hour drive. Plus another two hours from Norfolk to Glory. We can take turns driving. With luck we'll be home by two in the morning."

"This is a conspiracy," Daniel said. "You hate to fly. You like the idea of driving all the way back to North Carolina."

"There's no such thing as a one-woman conspiracy. Stop whining and start talking—I have a lot of catching up to do. And this is a perfect opportunity."

"Catching up about what?"

She leaned over and gave him a hug.

"About God!"

SIXTEEN

Daniel pushed the notes for his message to the side of his desk. He felt ready; he knew what he was going to say at today's Service of Thanksgiving. Nearly a month had passed since he and Lori had retrieved the church's gold—a month filled with astonishing changes at Glory Community Church.

His office door flew open. "Take a look outside, Daniel," Lori said excitedly. "We're going to have a standing room only today."

Daniel let Lori pull him to his feet and push him toward the window. There were dozens of people standing outside the church and the parking lot was already half full.

"Quite a turnout for a Saturday morning." He peered through the slatted Venetian blinds. "In fact, I see many faces that I don't recognize."

"Really?" Lori pushed down a slat and looked outside. "I think I know everyone out there."

Daniel let himself smile. Lori, a natural-born extrovert, had gotten to know most of Glory's population in days. He was still meeting people two years after arriving in town. Besides her outgoing personality, Lori had an uncanny ability to ask questions that got to the heart of other people's concerns. On more than one occasion, Daniel had to confess, she had helped him do a better job at pastoral care.

Lori is going to make a great pastor's wife.

The sound of determined knocking caught Daniel's attention. He turned away from the window and found Ann Trask standing in the doorway, a wholly business-like expression on her face. She held a sheaf of papers in her hand.

"Ann, I hope you aren't working today," he said.

"It's hardly work. A few essential details needed doing."

Daniel glanced at Lori, who was simultaneously shaking her head and rolling her eyes. They both were astonished at how quickly Ann Trask had become an indisputable workaholic. Now that Ann had a full-time job—manager of church administration—she apparently felt that every activity, every "detail" at Glory Community fell within her purview.

Ann moved next to Daniel's desk. "The first detail concerns both you and Lori—specifically, the trip you want to make to Chicago to meet Lori's parents." Ann paused while Daniel and Lori returned from the window. "As Lori knows, there are flights to Chicago from the airport in Norfolk, Virginia. However, I have discovered an alternative."

"Another airport?" Daniel asked.

"Another mode of transportation. You can travel to Chicago by train. You take the Carolinian from Rocky Mount, N.C., to Washington, D.C., stay overnight in Washington, and than travel to Chicago on the Cardinal."

"That's a two-and-a-half-day voyage instead of a two-and-a-half-hour flight," Daniel said, fighting to keep the panic out of his voice.

"I know," Lori said almost dreamily. "It sounds wonderful. I've always wanted to take an overnight train trip."

Daniel knew when arguing made no sense. "Well, I suppose a voyage would be fun."

Ann nodded. "Consider it arranged. Now, moving on to the next subject. Your wedding ceremony. I know that you're considering a wedding in the fall. Given the fact that both of you are retired U.S. Army officers, I thought that a military wedding might be appropriate.

Daniel noticed that Lori had become wide-eyed. "By military wedding," Lori said, "do you mean walking beneath an arch of sabers and wearing dress Army uniforms?"

Ann nodded again. "That's it."

Daniel bit back a laugh. He knew that Lori wanted to be married in a white wedding dress and that getting slapped on the backside by a saber after she walked beneath it was not part of her plans.

"Alas, Ann," Daniel said. "A military wedding is, as they say, an honor and a privilege for men and women currently serving in the military. We'll have to forego a military wedding in favor of a simple, civilian wedding."

Ann seemed disappointed as she walked off, but Lori gave him a big kiss.

"We've created a monster," she said.

"An efficient monster. She has Glory Community running like a well-oiled machine. I actually have more time these days to visit with members."

"You mean, she's kinda like a good top sergeant?"

"Exactly! That's a perfect description of her skills."

"Well, Colonel, we'd better get started mingling with your parishioners."

"Yes, Madam General."

"Hoo-rah!"

"You know, I've never learned to say that right."

"I'll have plenty of time to teach you—on our train ride to Chicago."

Daniel tried to tickle Lori's ribs, but she skedaddled out of the way.

Lori looked around the narthex. There were people everywhere—but much more importantly, they were *happy* people eager to give thanks to God. In recent months the church had been through enough tumult, enough crises, to tear a small congregation to shreds. Yet the fellowship had survived. Even Lori—a newcomer to Daniel's flock—recognized that the hand of God had been at work at Glory Community Church.

"Good morning, Detective Dorsett," a voice said behind her.

"Hello, George," she said as she spun around.

"We both seem to have new jobs in Glory. A little birdie told me that you will soon be our newest police person."

Lori smiled. It was impossible to keep secrets in a small town. She had agreed to join the Glory Police Department as a senior detective. Chief Porter had waived the requirement that new personnel attend the police academy because of her extensive experience as a U.S. Army CID Special Agent.

"Well, *if* that happens, it will be after Daniel and I are married."

"I'm already in my new job," George said proudly. "As you know, I've passed the mantle of financial secretary to Christine Stanton. I'm now head of the new members team.

"Glory Community is on a roll. We're definitely growing—and I expect to see lots more growth when people learn about our music mission work, our new, improved traditional and contemporary services."

"I hope George isn't boring you silly," Margo Ingles said. "I keep telling him that the Holy Spirit is in charge of church growth, not him. One day, it's bound to sink in."

Margo—a plump, vivacious woman with short, brown hair and large-framed eyeglasses—locked arms with George.

"Aha," Margo said to Lori, "you're wearing your new engagement ring. Let's see it."

Lori held out her hand. "How beautiful," Margo gushed, "an emerald-cut diamond in a gold solitaire setting."

"That's some sparkler!" George said. "We'd better check that all of the church's Gold Maple Leafs are accounted for."

Margo dug her elbow into George's side with enough force to elicit a loud, "Ouch!"

Lori giggled. Margo Ingles clearly understood George. And knew how to handle him.

"Come on, George," Margo said. "Let's find two seats together before they're all taken. I'd really hate to inflict you on anyone else."

Lori whispered an almost silent prayer of thanks as the Ingleses headed for the sanctuary. She preferred George Ingles in small doses.

When Lori turned again she saw Tony and Rebecca Taylor coming through the front door. True to her word, Rebecca had thrown a doozy of a welcome-home party for Tony at the Glory at Sea Marina—a festival of paper lanterns, loud music and good food. It seemed to Lori that most of the townsfolk had attended. By Tony's request, she and Daniel had received the first pieces of cake.

Lori waved. Rebecca hurried over, with Tony close behind. "We wanted you to be the first to know."

"I'm all ears," Lori said, excitedly.

"Well, tell her, Tony," Rebecca prompted.

"I've found *Marzipan II.*"

"She's really a wreck," Rebecca said with a wink.

"She won't be when I get through with her." Tony took Lori's hand. "She's a fantastic boat. A 1937 Hacker Craft Runabout. Twenty-four feet long. An absolute classic. Wait until you see her restored, complete with varnished mahogany topsides and green leather upholstery."

"Don't hold your breath," Rebecca said. "It's a humongous project."

"Nah!" Tony said. "Three years at most." He added, "I'll give you a call next week. I want to install a better alarm system at the marina. I'd like your advice." Lori knew why. Quentin Fisher had been able to get into Tony's office to plant the remote control transmitter and send the fax to himself on that fateful Thursday afternoon, when Rebecca and Tony had taken an afternoon off.

"You shall have it." Lori hugged both Taylors before they left to chitchat with other people.

"Do I get a hug, too?" Daniel asked as he sidled up to her.

"Nope. I'm saving that as your incentive to deliver a good message today."

"This congregation doesn't understand the different ways I suffer for them."

"Yeah, well, your suffering seems to be working. I

don't think I've ever seen so many smiling faces in one room. However…"

"There's a however?"

"Prepare yourself to encounter one not-so-smiling face here today. Kevin Pomeroy is coming."

"All the way from Chicago? I'm astounded."

"Actually, all the way from Richmond, Virginia. He's attending a security conference—still, it's nice of him to visit."

"How will I recognize him?"

"Fiftyish. Graying hair that's a getting thin on top. A little overweight." Her voice fell to a whisper, "Oh, look…there he is."

Kevin gave Lori her tenth hug of the morning, then he shook Daniel's hand after Lori introduced them.

"I've heard a lot about you," Daniel said.

"It's probably all true—unless you heard it from Lori."

"I want to thank you for firing her. Chicago's loss is definitely Glory's gain."

"Don't rub it in. She was my best investigator." He turned to Lori. "Admit it—you thought that I'd still be angry at you for not returning to Chicago."

"For a while—but I stopped worrying when I learned that you'd replaced me. I guess I'm not irreplaceable, after all."

"Maybe so, but you're definitely one of a kind. There will never be another Lori Dorsett."

Kevin handed her a thick envelope. "Here are all of the CDs you sent me. The photographs you took of Glory are yours. Use them in any way you wish."

Kevin hugged Lori again and left for the sanctuary.

Daniel put his arm around Lori's waist and squeezed. "I don't care what that man says, you're irreplaceable to me."

Ann Trask appeared, as if out of nowhere. "I'll take those photographs of Glory, if you please. I suspect they'll be perfect to use in our new church brochure. And we may even be able to lend a few to the Glory Chamber of Commerce. Did I tell you that I joined last week?"

Lori saw Daniel look away, his shoulders jiggling, as she gave Ann a crisp military salute.

Daniel took a deep breath. *Show time.* He slipped through the door and made his way to the front of the sanctuary. He touched Lori's shoulder as he passed by the front pew, where she was sitting in the seat next to the aisle.

He moved confidently to the pastor's lectern and nodded to Nina McEwen, Glory Community's director of music, who was seated at the church's brand-new electronic organ. Daniel gestured again and the congregation rose to its feet.

A series of commanding organ tones made most of the congregation gaze throughout the sanctuary for the source of the stunning sounds. An instant later the words to "A Mighty Fortress is Our God" appeared on the sanctuary's front walls. Only then did most of the congregants realize that projection screens had been cleverly camouflaged into the front walls.

Daniel suspected that Nina had chosen Martin Luther's famous hymn mostly as an opportunity to show off the new organ's great range and power. Nonetheless, the words were highly appropriate.

A mighty fortress is our God, a bulwark never failing;
Our helper He, amid the flood of mortal ills prevailing—

And…

*Did we in our own strength confide, our striving
would be losing;
Were not the right Man on our side, the Man of
God's own choosing—*

Daniel glanced at the choir. Tony Taylor and Rafe
Neilson stood next to each other, both singing fervent
baritone. Not far away, Emma Neilson stood in the
soprano section and Rebecca Taylor among the altos.
Another kind of peace had been restored to Glory: Rafe—
and Emma—had been forgiven for arresting Tony.

A familiar face toward the back of the sanctuary caught
Daniel's eye. Will Fisher. Daniel knew that Will was out
on bail and was scheduled to go to trial in mid-October.
He had received special permission to travel from New
York to North Carolina. He looked much healthier—and
happier—than when Daniel had last seen him.

In Daniel's mind, the most extraordinary thing about
Will Fisher was that God had used him to bring Lori
Dorsett back to Him.

Daniel heard Lori singing enthusiastically, almost in
tune.

*And though this world, with devils filled, should
threaten to undo us,
We will not fear, for God hath willed His truth to
triumph through us—*

Daniel considered the truth of these words written

nearly five hundred years ago. We were almost undone by the world and its devils. Praise God, Your truth triumphed through us.

When the singing ended, Daniel turned on his wireless microphone and looked out at his congregation.

"Please pray with me. Lord, thank You for this day. Thank You for Your blessings poured down on Your church. We ask You to be with us in the future as we move forward to do Your will. In Jesus' name, Amen."

Daniel paused for dramatic effect. "Sometimes, my friends, things aren't what they seem—and it's a good thing. This sanctuary is an excellent example. It has been modified in a way that gives us an advanced speaker system that will serve both our new electronic organ and our new contemporary sound system. Because our two teams worked together, most of the technology is hidden, leaving our sanctuary looking like it always did. Well done!

"Other times, things aren't what they seem because we've put the wrong labels on them. A firefly is not a fly, it's a kind of beetle. And despite it's name, a lead pencil contains graphite, not lead. And most of us know that a peanut is a legume—a member of the pea and bean family—not a nut. Mistakes like this often happen out of carelessness. One of my favorite tales is about Francisco Fernandez de Cordoba, a Spanish explorer who landed on the Caribbean coast of Mexico in 1517. When he asked the local Mayans for the name of the region, they answered, Yucatan. Francisco duly noted the 'name' not realizing that 'Yucatan' is the Mayan phrase for 'I don't understand what you just said!'"

Daniel expected a laugh at this point and got one. When the congregation settled down, he continued. "But many times, when things aren't what they seem—well, it may be that someone is trying to fool us. During the past months, Glory Community Church, its staff and its members have experienced many things that were not what they seemed.

"The Bible emphasizes the need for discernment in spiritual matters—but I say we also need discernment in our daily lives. We need to listen to the Holy Spirit before we act, both spiritually and in our everyday dealings. And we also need to exercise our own common sense."

Daniel paused again and looked at the expectant faces tilted toward him. "I'm reminded of an ancient proverb from the Middle East—Trust God, but tie up your camel."

"I recognize that parable," Will said to Lori. "The shepherd will do whatever it takes to find the one lost sheep—even if he has to leave the other ninety-nine alone for a while."

Lori smiled at him. "It makes me think of you and me." She added, "No wonder that's become my favorite of the five stained-glass windows."

"They're all really pretty. They make the inside of the sanctuary glow when the sun is shining."

"Don't remind me!" Lori made a face. "I've promised to take inside pictures of them, but I haven't had a free moment to set up my new camera."

"Speaking of free moments—" Will glanced at his watch "—I have to hurry to catch my flight home, or else I'll turn into a jailhouse pumpkin."

She gave him a goodbye hug.

That must be hug number one hundred. Ah well, hugging comes with the territory.

She sat in the first pew in the sanctuary, alone for the first time in hours.

"Don't get too comfortable," Daniel said from the doorway. "I'm here for the hug you promised me."

"Not *another* hug. I'm genuinely hugged out."

"Okay. I'll settle for a big kiss."

"This is a church sanctuary! Is kissing allowed?"

Daniel sat next to her and pulled her close.

"Kissing in the sanctuary happens at least once after every wedding."

"Oh!" Lori said. "That's true. We're merely conducting a preview."

Lori let Daniel tilt her face toward him. When he kissed her, she kissed him back.

Dear Reader,

Gone to Glory is our second cozy mystery set in Glory, North Carolina—a typical small Southern town that should be a haven for gentle living. But towns of any size can harbor ugly secrets. And those secrets can sometimes lead to violent death.

Lori Dorsett came to Glory as an investigator on a secret mission. She saw herself as a "good guy," a person seeking to learn the truth and advance the cause of justice. But to get the job done, Lori was fully prepared to betray the trust of the people she dealt with. To Lori, the ends justified the means—no matter who she hurt in the process.

As Christians, we love the truth and strive to see justice done. But what if our efforts in those directions force us to deceive others, to lie, to take advantage of them? Is it ever right to achieve good by doing bad?

Lori was driven to ask herself questions like these when she fell in love with Reverend Daniel Hartman—one of the townsfolk she'd deceived. For the first time in her career she began to understand the full impact of her lies and deceptions on innocent people. And the discoveries she made about herself helped renew her faith as a Christian.

Eventually Lori found a better path to truth and justice— a path that didn't clash with her newfound faith. And along the way, she managed to deliver an extraordinary blessing to her new friends at Glory Community Church.

We hope you enjoyed this second visit to Glory as much as we did. Let's meet again soon in the town that's famous for the Glorious SOGgy Burger.

Ron and Janet Benrey

QUESTIONS FOR DISCUSSION

1. In order to do her job properly, Lori must present herself to the people of Glory as someone she's not. Have you ever been placed in a similar situation? What did you do? How would you reconcile your "workplace" self with your Christian self if you were in Lori's shoes?

2. Loyalty is a trait we all admire. Has being loyal to one person caused you to lose the confidence and affection of others? How did you handle it?

3. As Christians, we are told not to lie. But sometimes our jobs require that we not be completely truthful with others. Companies have secrets that they can't share. Has a company secret ever forced you to be less than honest with a family member?

4. Lori initially presents herself to the people of Glory as a ditz. Do the people you meet always meet the true you? Or do you put on a public face when introduced to new people? How long does it normally take for you to feel comfortable sharing yourself with new people in your life?

5. George Ingles may have been in over his head when it came to choosing the right investment for Glory Community Church. Have you ever been in over your head in a work situation? How did you handle it? Did you seek help or try to muddle through by yourself, hoping for the best?

6. If you had a job you really hated, but it paid well, how long would you remain in that position? Would earning good money ever be enough to keep you working somewhere unpleasant?

7. When Lori begins to like the people of Glory, she decides that she must do the right thing by them. Were you ever in a situation like Lori's where you felt compelled to do the right thing, even though it would mean being disloyal to your friends or your company?

8. Will Fisher turned out to be a gambling addict. There are many addictions—some may even look good to others, such as being a workaholic. Have you ever been addicted to your work? Or to a sport? Or a television program? Are you still addicted? And if not, how did you break it? What role did faith play in your being healed? Was your church family able to help?

9. The Bible teaches us to not be "unequally yoked" with a nonbeliever. Daniel Hartman was willing to give Lori up. But she had a change of heart. Have you left a relationship because of your faith? How did you heal? Looking back on your decision, can you see God's hand in it?

10. What does your being a Christian mean to your co-workers? Do they know what you believe? Do they see your faith in action?

REQUEST YOUR FREE BOOKS!

2 FREE RIVETING INSPIRATIONAL NOVELS PLUS 2 FREE MYSTERY GIFTS

Love Inspired®
SUSPENSE

YES! Please send me 2 FREE Love Inspired® Suspense novels and my 2 FREE mystery gifts. After receiving them, if I don't wish to receive any more books, I can return the shipping statement marked "cancel." If I don't cancel, I will receive 4 brand-new novels every month and be billed just $3.99 per book in the U.S. or $4.74 per book in Canada, plus 25¢ shipping and handling per book and applicable taxes, if any*. That's a savings of 20% off the cover price! I understand that accepting the 2 free books and gifts places me under no obligation to buy anything. I can always return a shipment and cancel at any time. Even if I never buy another book from Steeple Hill, the two free books and gifts are mine to keep forever.

123 IDN EL5H   323 IDN ELQH

Name	(PLEASE PRINT)
Address	Apt. #
City	State/Prov.	Zip/Postal Code

Signature (if under 18, a parent or guardian must sign)

Order online at www.LoveInspiredSuspense.com

Or mail to Steeple Hill Reader Service™:

IN U.S.A.: P.O. Box 1867, Buffalo, NY 14240-1867
IN CANADA: P.O. Box 609, Fort Erie, Ontario L2A 5X3

Not valid to current Love Inspired Suspense subscribers.

Want to try two free books from another series?
Call 1-800-873-8635 or visit www.morefreebooks.com

* Terms and prices subject to change without notice. NY residents add applicable sales tax. Canadian residents will be charged applicable provincial taxes and GST. This offer is limited to one order per household. All orders subject to approval. Credit or debit balances in a customer's account(s) may be offset by any other outstanding balance owed by or to the customer. Please allow 4 to 6 weeks for delivery.

Your Privacy: Steeple Hill is committed to protecting your privacy. Our Privacy Policy is available online at www.eHarlequin.com or upon request from the Reader Service. From time to time we make our lists of customers available to reputable firms who may have a product or service of interest to you. If you would ~efer we not share your name and address, please check here. ☐

LISUS07

Love Inspired.
SUSPENSE

TITLES AVAILABLE NEXT MONTH

Don't miss these four stories in October

SHADOWS IN THE MIRROR by Linda Hall
Her aunt warned her against returning to Burlington,
but Marylee Simson had to know why her parents' very
existence seemed shrouded in mystery...and whether
handsome Evan Baxter could be linked to the tragic accident
that had claimed them.

BURIED SECRETS by Margaret Daley
Fresh from her grandfather's funeral, Maggie Somers
was stunned to find his home ransacked and her family's
nemesis, Zach Collier, amid the wreckage. Could she believe
his warning that the thieves would certainly target her next?

FROM THE ASHES by Sharon Mignerey
Angela London was haunted by her dark past. Now a guide-
dog trainer working with former football star Brian Ramsey,
she needed to thwart a vengeful enemy to protect her
newfound happiness.

BAYOU JUSTICE by Robin Caroll
With an angry past dividing their families, CoCo LeBlanc's
discovery of her former fiancé's father's body in the bayou
put her name at the top of the suspect list. Working with her
ex to clear both their names, could she survive the Cajun
killer's next attack?